Mysteries according to Humphrey

For more **Humphrey** adventures, look for

1
The World
According to Humphrey

2
Friendship
According to Humphrey

3
Trouble
According to Humphrey

4
Surprises
According to Humphrey

5
Adventure
According to Humphrey

6
Summer
According to Humphrey

7
School Days
According to Humphrey

Mysteries according to Humphrey

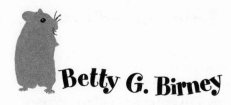

Betty G. Birney

G. P. Putnam's Sons
An Imprint of Penguin Group (USA) Inc.

G. P. PUTNAM'S SONS
A division of Penguin Young Readers Group.
Published by The Penguin Group.
Penguin Group (USA) Inc., 375 Hudson Street, New York, NY 10014, U.S.A.
Penguin Group (Canada), 90 Eglinton Avenue East, Suite 700, Toronto, Ontario M4P 2Y3,
Canada (a division of Pearson Penguin Canada Inc.).
Penguin Books Ltd, 80 Strand, London WC2R 0RL, England.
Penguin Ireland, 25 St. Stephen's Green, Dublin 2, Ireland (a division of Penguin Books Ltd).
Penguin Group (Australia), 250 Camberwell Road, Camberwell, Victoria 3124,
Australia (a division of Pearson Australia Group Pty Ltd).
Penguin Books India Pvt Ltd, 11 Community Centre, Panchsheel Park,
New Delhi—110 017, India.
Penguin Group (NZ), 67 Apollo Drive, Rosedale, Auckland 0632, New Zealand
(a division of Pearson New Zealand Ltd).
Penguin Books (South Africa) (Pty) Ltd, 24 Sturdee Avenue, Rosebank,
Johannesburg 2196, South Africa.
Penguin Books Ltd, Registered Offices: 80 Strand, London WC2R 0RL, England.

Published simultaneously in Canada.
Printed in the United States of America.
Design by Anne Ericsson. Text set in Stempel Schneidler.

Library of Congress Cataloging-in-Publication Data
Birney, Betty G. Mysteries according to Humphrey / Betty G. Birney
p. cm.—(Humphrey adventures)
Summary: After learning about Sherlock Holmes, Humphrey the classroom hamster
follows clues to try and discover why Mrs. Brisbane is gone and Mr. E., a fun but not
very educational substitute, is taking her place in Room 26 at Longfellow School.
[1. Hamsters—Fiction. 2. Substitute teachers—Fiction. 3. Schools—Fiction. 4. Mystery
and detective stories.] 1. Title. PZ7.B5229Mys 2012 [E]—dc23 2011020075

ISBN 978-0-399-25414-7
1 3 5 7 9 10 8 6 4 2

In memory of Humphrey's #1 fan,
Sarah Williams

"Sweet-Sarah"

Contents

The Case of the Mysterious Detective

Outside, the sun was shining, but inside Room 26 of Longfellow School, it was a dark and stormy night.

Mrs. Brisbane, our teacher, was reading us a fur-raising mystery story from a big red book.

A mystery is like a puzzle. It can be something un-squeakably scary, like a thing that goes THUMP in the night.

Or a mystery can be something ordinary, like what happened to Mrs. Brisbane's glasses. Sometimes our teacher can't find her glasses when they're right on her head.

Even though my classmates and I can read by our-selves, we love having Mrs. Brisbane read to us. (It *is* surprising that I can read, because I am the classroom hamster, but I am also SMART-SMART-SMART, if I do say so myself.)

As I listened, I climbed up to the tippy top of my cage and looked out at my classmates. When school started in September, they were *all* mysteries to me. I didn't realize that at the beginning of the school year, a new class comes in. A class of *total strangers*.

It's taken me a while to figure out why Hurry-Up-Harry is late so often and why Slow-Down-Simon moves so fast. I learned that Rolling-Rosie's wheelchair doesn't slow her down a bit. And I learned that Helpful-Holly is sometimes *Too*-Helpful-Holly.

Now it's October. I'm still getting to know some of the students who sit on the opposite side of the room from my cage. I haven't figured out why Do-It-Now-Daniel Dee always puts things off and why Stop-Talking-Sophie Kaminski has so much trouble being quiet.

In time, I hope I'll solve those mysteries, too. I guess being a classroom hamster is a lot like being a detective.

A detective is someone who solves mysteries. The story Mrs. Brisbane was reading was about a detective named Sherlock Holmes, who was one smart human. In his picture on the cover of the red book, he wore a strange-looking hat. Mrs. Brisbane said it was called a deerstalker hat. She also said he sometimes played the violin to help him think. (Which made me wish I had a violin of my own.)

There were a lot of stories in the book. This puzzling mystery had to do with a man with flaming red hair, named Mr. Jabez Wilson. He came to Sherlock Holmes and explained something strange that had happened to him. It started when he saw an ad in the newspaper for a job that was *only* for a person with flaming red hair. I guess that's why the name of the story was "The Adventure of the Red-Headed League."

Mrs. Brisbane asked us, "Why would they only want someone with red hair?"

Kelsey Kirkpatrick's hand shot up so fast, she almost hit Just-Joey, who sat next to her.

"Please Be-Careful-Kelsey," Mrs. Brisbane said. "So what do you think?"

Kelsey said, "They must be looking for somebody smart! Everybody knows that redheads are the smartest people!"

My classmates all laughed, because Kelsey has red hair. Naturally, she would think red-haired people are the smartest.

Mrs. Brisbane laughed, too. "Yes, Kelsey. Some red-haired people are very smart. But I don't think that was the reason."

She asked if we had any other ideas.

I thought and thought. If the job needed someone smart, I think they might look for a clever hamster, like me.

Paul Fletcher, whom I think of as Small-Paul, had another idea. "Maybe they needed someone who looked like someone else . . . a different person with red hair?" he suggested.

"That's an interesting idea, Paul. You'd make a good detective," Mrs. Brisbane said.

Paul Green, whom I think of as Tall-Paul, raised his

hand. "Maybe the person has to wear a costume," he suggested, "and they need red hair to go with the costume."

"Excellent idea," Mrs. Brisbane said.

Thomas T. True looked puzzled and he raised his hand. "Is this a true story?" he asked. "I mean, is Sherlock Holmes a real person?"

Mrs. Brisbane smiled. "No, it's a made-up story. But Sherlock Holmes almost seems like a real person, and he's been popular for many years. When he solves a mystery, he looks for clues."

She explained that a clue is information that helps you solve a mystery. And Sherlock Holmes was always looking for clues, because a good detective always has to be sharp-eyed.

Mrs. Brisbane read some more. The red-haired man got hired, but it turned out that the job was nothing more than copying out the encyclopedia every evening.

What a strange job! Why would anyone need someone to copy the encyclopedia? And why would the person have to have red hair?

This was a mystery, indeed!

Suddenly, Mrs. Brisbane stopped reading and closed the book.

"Eeek!" I squeaked. My classmates all groaned and begged her to read more, but it was almost time for afternoon recess.

"When you come back, I'll have a different kind of mystery for you," she said, which got us all excited again.

Soon, the classroom was empty, except for Og the Frog and me. (Classroom pets like us don't get to go outside for recess.)

Once we were alone, I squeaked to my neighbor, who lives in a tank next to my cage. "Og, why do you think that ad asked for someone with red hair?"

He splashed around a little in the water side of his tank and then leaped up and said, "BOING-BOING!"

He sounds like a broken guitar string, but he can't help it. It's just the sound he makes.

I guess Og doesn't know much about red hair. He doesn't have any hair or fur at all. And he's VERY-VERY-VERY green.

"I don't have any ideas, either," I said. "But I'm sure going to think about it."

When my friends came back, they were anxious to hear about the *other* mystery.

"You know, class, when we read, we're all detectives," the teacher said.

We all looked puzzled.

"Sometimes we come across a word we don't know, right?" she asked.

Everyone nodded, including me.

"So to figure out what the word means, we look for a clue," Mrs. Brisbane continued. "Just like Sherlock Holmes. Try this sentence."

Then Mrs. Brisbane wrote something very mysterious on the board.

**The twins looked so much alike, I was piewhacked
when I tried to tell them apart.**

Piewhacked? That word had never been on our vocabulary list.

Lots of my friends giggled when they saw the word.

"Who knows what *piewhacked* means?" Mrs. Brisbane asked.

Thomas raised his hand. "I think it means 'hit someone in the face with a pie.'"

Everybody laughed, including me. But that didn't make much sense in the sentence about the twins.

"Let's try again," Mrs. Brisbane said. She wrote another sentence.

**The rules of soccer can be very piewhacking if
you've never seen a game before.**

This time, more students giggled.

Piewhacked? Piewhacking? What was she trying to say? Were the pies flying at the soccer game?

"Look at how the word is used in the sentences to get some clues," she told us.

Mrs. Brisbane wrote one more sentence on the board.

**When the teacher put the wrong answers on
the board, there was a lot of piewhacksion in
the classroom.**

Piewhacksion? Was there a pie fight in the classroom? Or had my teacher lost her mind?

"I'm confused!" I blurted out, even though all that my human friends heard was "SQUEAK!"

"Confusion!" Slow-Down-Simon shouted.

I'm sorry to say he forgot to raise his hand before speaking.

"Confused!" Too-Helpful-Holly said. She raised her hand, but she didn't wait for the teacher to call on her before speaking.

"Let's see if that word works," Mrs. Brisbane said with a smile. "'The twins looked so much alike, I was *confused* when I tried to tell them apart.'"

That worked for me.

"How about 'The rules of soccer can be very *confusing* if you've never seen a game before,'" she continued. "And finally, 'When the teacher put the wrong answers on the board, there was a lot of *confusion* in the classroom.'"

Now I was pawsitive that *piewhack* meant *confuse*.

"For your homework tonight, here are five more mystery words to figure out," she said as she handed Rolling-Rosie the homework sheets to pass out.

Unfortunately, Rosie didn't give me one, so I couldn't see what the mystery words were.

I tried making up my own mystery words, like *flapple* and *scarrot*, but they just made me hungry!

⌒·⌒

At the end of the day, just before the bell rang, the door to Room 26 swung open and in walked Mrs. Wright, the physical education teacher. She was clutching a pink jacket and, as usual, wore a shiny silver whistle on a cord around her neck.

Mrs. Wright likes to blow that whistle, and when she does, it makes my ears wiggle and the fur on my neck stand up. It's LOUD-LOUD-LOUD. Way too loud for the small, sensitive ears of a hamster.

Mrs. Wright also likes rules. Okay, she *loves* rules.

I can understand why someone who teaches children to play games would love rules, because rules are very important to games. But to squeak the truth, I think she loves rules just a tiny bit too much, and I think Mrs. Brisbane agrees with me.

"Yes, Mrs. Wright?" our teacher asked.

Mrs. Wright raised the pink jacket up high. "I believe this belongs to one of your students," she said. "Normally, I would put it in the lost and found in my office. But her name was inside and I thought she might need it. It's quite chilly out there. Phoebe Pratt?"

Poor Forgetful-Phoebe looked embarrassed as she walked over to get the jacket. "Sorry, Mrs. Wright," she said.

"Students must be responsible for their belongings," Mrs. Wright said. "You'd be amazed at what treasures I have in the lost and found."

"Thank you, Mrs. Wright," Mrs. Brisbane replied.

Mrs. Wright paused at the door and fingered her whistle. I steeled myself for a loud blast, but luckily, she walked out the door silently.

Thomas T. True waved his hand and Mrs. Brisbane called on him.

"Don't go to that lost and found," he said. "I went there last year and it was a scary place."

"Now, what was scary about it?" Mrs. Brisbane asked.

Thomas's eyes grew wide. "There were creepy things like spiderwebs and . . . claws!"

I felt a shiver. Some of my classmates giggled.

"Oh, and a dead snake." Thomas stopped and thought. "Maybe it was alive. And I'm pretty sure I saw a severed hand."

I felt a quiver. There were gasps and more giggles and some of my friends went, "Ewwww."

Mrs. Brisbane walked between the tables toward Thomas. "Are you sure that's true?"

"Yes, ma'am," he said. "At least that's what I remember."

"Well, I don't think Mrs. Wright would keep any of those things in her lost and found," Mrs. Brisbane said. "Maybe you just imagined it."

Thomas thought for a second. "Maybe, but I don't think so."

Suddenly, the bell rang and my friends jumped up from their chairs.

Slow-Down-Simon was the first one out the door, and my other friends were close behind him.

After all of my classmates had left Room 26, Mrs. Wright came back in.

"That Phoebe is quite forgetful," she said. "Have you noticed?"

"Yes, I have. We're working on it," Mrs. Brisbane said.

I'd certainly figured out that Phoebe had a problem remembering things like homework and lunches. But I hadn't figured out why. All I really knew about Phoebe was that she lived with her grandmother, who seemed like an unsqueakably nice human.

Mrs. Wright nodded politely and headed for the door. But before she left, she turned and said, "Please try to encourage your students to visit the lost and found. It's right in my office, inside the gym."

"I'll do that," Mrs. Brisbane said.

Mrs. Brisbane tidied up her desk for a few minutes. Then she wandered over to the table where Og and I live, next to the window. "Have a good night, fellows," she said. "I hope today wasn't too *piewhacking* for you. See you in the morning."

She laughed and then she left, just like on any other day.

"See you in the morning." That's what she said.

I remember it so well.

❧

Later that night, Aldo came in to clean the classroom, as he does every night.

"Never fear, Aldo's here!" he boomed. Then he laughed, which made his big, furry mustache shake.

10

He went right to work, moving the tables and sweeping the floors, humming a happy-sounding song. When he got close to Mrs. Brisbane's desk, he stopped and picked up the red book.

"Hey, Sherlock Holmes! I love these stories," he said, thumbing through the pages. "I remember that one about the redheaded guy."

"Tell me what happens!" I shouted.

Even Og splashed around in his tank. "BOING-BOING!" he twanged.

"Sorry I don't have time to read it to you," he told us. "Too bad you can't read it yourself."

Aldo probably knows me better than any of my human friends, but even he doesn't know that I can read. It's not easy for a small hamster to read a BIG-BIG-BIG book. That's why I like it when Mrs. Brisbane reads to us. I decided I could wait until the next day to hear her read more of "The Red-Headed League." But it was nice to know that Aldo liked Sherlock Holmes as much as I do.

After Aldo left, the room was silent. Og didn't splash. He didn't even say "BOING!"

What was he thinking about? We're good friends, but Og will always be a mystery to me.

Humans are also very mysterious to me. I've learned a lot about them, but there are still so many things I don't understand. I took out the little notebook I keep hidden behind my mirror and started scribbling in it with my tiny pencil.

Mysteries about humans:

- *Why do they keep odd and unpleasant pets like dogs and cats when they could have a very nice hamster . . . like me?*
- *Why do they throw bits of leftover food away when they could store it like I do—in my bedding or in my cheek pouch?*
- *Where <u>are</u> humans' cheek pouches?*
- *Why do humans laugh when they talk about poo? Especially my poo?*

Mysteries about frogs:

- *Why don't frogs have fur? Or even hair?*
- *Why can't frogs act just a little bit more like hamsters?*

I wasn't sure those mysteries would ever be solved.

HUMPHREY'S DETECTIONARY: Even smart detectives like Sherlock Holmes can't solve a mystery without a clue.

The Case of the Missing Mrs.

I'm always excited for the start of a new day in Room 26. But the next morning, I could hardly wait to hear Mrs. Brisbane read more about Sherlock Holmes.

I waited for the key to turn in the door and for Mrs. Brisbane to bustle into the classroom.

I waited for the bell to ring and for my friends to arrive.

I waited and waited and waited some more. In fact, I waited so long, the bell rang, but *nobody* came in.

I knew it wasn't Saturday. I never spend Saturdays at school because I go home with one of my classmates on the weekends. Sometimes I go home with Mrs. Brisbane. Either way, I have a hamster-iffic good time. (Og usually stays in Room 26 on the weekends, which must be lonely for him, poor frog.)

"Og, something's wrong!" I squeaked loudly to my neighbor.

"BOING-BOING-BOING-BOING-BOING!" he replied. He sounded as worried as I was.

I could see some of my friends' faces looking through the window in the door.

"Humphrey, let us in," I heard Simon's muffled voice calling.

It was the only time in my life I wished I wasn't a hamster so I could be big enough to open that door.

Long after the bell rang, I finally heard some jiggling and joggling and the door swung open at last!

But Mrs. Brisbane wasn't the human opening the door. It was our principal, Mr. Morales. Behind him were my fellow students.

"Come on in, boys and girls," he said.

Mr. Morales is the Most Important Person at Longfellow School because he's in charge of everything. He was wearing a tie with tiny little question marks all over it. He has *lots* of interesting ties.

"Take your seats," he said.

My fellow students were worried, too. I could tell, because they were quieter than usual. (I guess that was a clue.)

"It looks as if Mrs. Brisbane is going to be late," he said. "We're trying to reach her now."

Mrs. Brisbane is NEVER-NEVER-NEVER late. This was a very *piewhacking* morning.

"I'll take attendance," Mr. Morales said.

Holly jumped up and offered to help.

"Thank you," he said to her. "But I think I can handle it."

Then he called out names and each student answered "Present" in return.

Everyone was present *except* Mrs. Brisbane.

Mr. Morales looked uneasy. "So, what do you usually do first in the morning?"

Helpful-Holly raised her hand. "We had homework last night," she said. "I can collect it."

"Thank you," Mr. Morales said.

Holly went up and down the aisles collecting the homework. How I wished I could get a look at those five mystery words!

Everybody turned in a homework sheet except for one person: Forgetful-Phoebe. When Holly passed by her table, Phoebe blushed and said, "Oh, no! I forgot it! I'll bring it tomorrow."

As helpful as Holly is, she sometimes gets carried away. That's when I call her Too-Helpful-Holly. She frowned and said, "You were supposed to bring it *today*."

Mr. Morales stepped forward. "It's okay, Holly. We'll straighten things out when Mrs. Brisbane gets here," he said.

Whew! I was GLAD-GLAD-GLAD to hear him say that Mrs. Brisbane was coming.

Just then, the phone in the classroom rang. Mr. Morales said, "Oh," and then, "I see," and finally, "Very well," while my classmates were completely quiet.

Mr. Morales hung up the phone. "Boys and girls, Mrs. Brisbane won't be here today," he said. "A substitute is on the way to take care of the class."

The last time I'd had a substitute teacher was when

Ms. Mac was here. But I didn't know she was a substitute, because I didn't know much about school when I first arrived. I've certainly learned a lot since then!

Mr. Morales seemed a little confused about what to do next and he kept looking at his watch.

"Read to us—from 'The Red-Headed League'!" I squeaked loudly.

My classmates all giggled when they heard me.

Mr. Morales walked over to my cage. "Oh, so you want to take over the class, Humphrey?" he said.

I jumped on my wheel and spun it fast.

"Maybe Humphrey thinks we should do some exercise," Mr. Morales said.

That made my classmates giggle even more.

Rosie made her wheelchair spin in a circle. "I love to spin, too," she said, and everybody laughed.

Just then, the door to the classroom opened and a young man rushed into the room.

The first thing I noticed about him was his red hair. (I think Sherlock Holmes would have noticed that, too.)

I also saw that he was wearing round glasses, and on his shirt was a big button with writing on it that said *Give Peas a Chance*.

I love any veggies, including peas, so this human and I definitely had something in common.

He had a big cloth bag slung over his shoulder, sort of like Santa Claus. It was lumpy and bumpy and way too big for a lunch bag!

Mr. Morales stepped forward and shook his hand. "Welcome. I'm the principal," he said. "Mr. Morales."

"Hi," the young man said. "Ed Edonopolous."

The principal turned to the class and said, "Here's your substitute for today. I expect you to give him your full attention."

Mr. Morales left and Mr. Edonopolous gave us a friendly smile. "Hi, kids," he said. "I know Edonopolous is a mouthful, so you can call me Mr. E."

There were a few giggles and Slow-Down-Simon repeated the name out loud the way I'd heard it: "Mystery!"

Mr. E. smiled and nodded. "Mystery! That's a good one. Hey, you know my name, but I don't know yours. I'm going to come up and down the aisles and you tell me who you are."

He walked around the students' tables, one by one, asking, "What's your name?"

He high-fived each student and said something like, "Cool shirt," or, "Glad to know you," or, "Awesome."

"My name is Holly and I collected the homework this morning," Too-Helpful-Holly said when Mr. E. got to her. "It was our mystery words sheet. I put it on the teacher's desk. Only one didn't get turned in."

"Uh, thanks," Mr. E. said.

"I'm Sophie and I really like your pin. I like to wear pins with sayings, too," Stop-Talking-Sophie said. "Do you remember where you got it?"

17

Mr. E. didn't remember where he got it. Sophie kept on talking until he said, "I think I'd better give the rest of the class a chance."

He moved on to the next table.

"I'm Thomas T. True," Thomas said. "My dad's a detective. Like Sherlock Holmes!"

"Not," I heard Just-Joey mutter.

Mr. E. turned toward the class. "What's the problem?" he asked.

"He told me that his dad's an airplane pilot," Just-Joey said.

"So?" Thomas said. "He can be both."

"He told *me* that his dad's a ship captain," Small-Paul grumbled.

Mr. E. just laughed. "Sounds like a talented father." Then he moved on again.

When he got to my side of the room, he finally noticed Og and me.

"Whoa," he said. "These are some funny-looking students."

I heard some giggles, but I wasn't laughing. I can see how you might call Og funny-looking, but not a handsome Golden Hamster like me!

Mr. E. leaned in and looked right at me. "What's its name?"

"Humphrey!" I squeaked loudly. "And I am not an *it*!"

"Whoa," he said again. "I think he's talking. What is he—a rat?"

It was clear that this teacher didn't do his homework

when it came to animals. Imagine, mistaking me for a rat!

Luckily, my friends all shouted out, "Hamster!"

"His name is Humphrey," Holly added.

Mr. E. said, "Cool." Then he turned to Og. "I know this is a frog—right? What's its name?" he asked.

"BOING-BOING-BOING!" Og twanged loudly. He probably doesn't like being called an "it" either.

"His name is Og," Rolling-Rosie explained.

"Og the Frog," Mr. E. said. "I like it."

He was quiet for a few seconds as he looked around the room. "You know, I was still sleeping when I got the call to come over here, so I don't know what your teacher's plans were today," he said. "Why don't you tell me what *you* want to do?"

My friends looked surprised. I'm sure I looked surprised, too.

Hurry-Up-Harry waved his hand and Mr. E. called on him.

"I'd like to go home!" he said.

Everybody laughed. It was a funny thing to say. But I don't think Mrs. Brisbane would have laughed.

"I understand," Mr. E. said. "But I don't think that's going to happen. Hey, I know . . . why don't we sing a song to help me remember your names?"

Everybody seemed to like the idea of a song.

I was amazed at what happened next. Mr. E. pointed at a student. The student stood up and said his name and then the teacher made a little rhyming song with the name. He took parts of each name and added things to it, like "banana fana" and "fee fi fo." After a few names, the whole class joined in.

The song made my friends giggle, but it was very confusing to me. After he'd finished the whole class, Rosie raised her hand and asked if they could do *my* name.

I can't remember it all but it ended with:

Fee fi mo Mumphrey,

Humphrey!

Bumphrey-Mumphrey-Fumphrey—whoa! How was this going to help him remember our real names?

Og's name sounded even stranger: Bog, Fog, Mog.

I don't know what Og thought, but I was in a bit of a fog myself! I was still thinking about Mumphrey and Mog when the bell rang for recess.

As soon as my classmates were gone, Mr. E. picked up his big sack and looked inside. "Let's see," he mumbled. "What next? Maybe this."

Then he glanced over at Og and me and chuckled. "I don't know why I'm talking out loud when I know you can't understand me."

Og piped up first. "BOING-BOING."

"You are WRONG-WRONG-WRONG!" I squeaked, wishing with all my might that Mr. E. could understand me.

He didn't notice. He was too busy rummaging around in that big cloth sack.

Suddenly, he stopped and smiled. "Okay. I've got it!"

That's all he said.

I thought I'd pretty well figured out humans in my time as a classroom hamster so far. But Mr. E. was a real mystery to me.

～•～

When my friends were back in their seats, Mr. E. announced that it was time for math.

Some of the students groaned, until the teacher reached into his bag and pulled out a basketball.

"We're going to play a game," he said. "It's called Mathketball!"

My friends looked puzzled. I didn't blame them.

"Of course, we could just have a math quiz," Mr. E. said. "If you'd like."

"No!" the students all yelled. "Mathketball!"

Mumphrey. Mog. Mathketball—all mystery words. I was learning a whole new language today.

First, Mr. E. threw the ball to Slow-Down-Simon. "Quick! Four plus four."

Simon caught the ball and said, "Eight!"

"Great," Mr. E. said. "But in Mathketball, instead of saying the answer, you bounce it."

Simon looked confused for a second and then he understood. He bounced the basketball one-two-three-four-five-six-seven-eight times.

"That's it," Mr. E. told him. "Now throw it back."

The teacher caught the ball and threw it to Be-Careful-Kelsey. "Ten minus five," he said.

Kelsey bounced the ball one-two-three-four-five times.

"Great," Mr. E. said. "Now throw it back."

Kelsey dropped the ball and it bounced across the floor.

"Careful," Mr. E. said as he scooped it up.

Just-Joey caught the ball next and when Mr. E. said, "Twelve plus three," Joey bounced it one-two-three-four-five-six-seven-eight-nine-ten-eleven-twelve-thirteen-fourteen-fifteen times. I know because I counted!

Then the ball went to Paul G. "Six plus five," Mr. E. said.

Tall-Paul bounced it one-two-three-four-five-six-seven-eight-nine-ten times. Then he stopped.

"One more time!" I squeaked. I guess he didn't hear me.

Mr. E. gave him another chance, which was nice, and Tall-Paul got the problem right.

As the game went on, the pace went faster and faster. As it got more exciting, it also got louder and louder.

And then . . . the door to Room 26 swung open. Standing in the doorway was Mrs. Wright.

Mr. E. looked pretty surprised when he saw her. Maybe he noticed her whistle. I certainly did.

"Hello?" he said. It was more a question than a greeting.

"You're the substitute for Mrs. Brisbane?" she asked.

"Yep. I'm Mr. E.," the substitute said.

Mrs. Wright looked puzzled. "Mr. E.?" she asked. "That's your name?"

Mr. E. laughed. "My name is Edonopolous, but Mr. E. is fine with me."

Mrs. Wright frowned. I guess Mr. E. wasn't fine with her.

"And you are . . . ?" Mr. E. asked.

"Mrs. Wright," the PE teacher answered.

To my GREAT-GREAT-GREAT surprise, Mr. E. laughed. "Mrs. Wright? I guess you're never wrong!"

Some of my classmates giggled, but Mrs. Wright wasn't the giggling type. She stepped into the classroom and looked around.

"Is that basketball the property of Longfellow School?" she asked.

The substitute shook his head. "Nope. I brought it from home."

That didn't seem to please Mrs. Wright at all. "You're probably not aware that basketballs are only allowed outside on the playground. No ball-playing in the classroom," she said. "And only official Longfellow School equipment is allowed."

"Really?" Mr. E. seemed surprised.

"Really," Mrs. Wright said. "I'm the chairperson of the Committee for School Property. There are safety issues with having a ball in the classroom. And by the way, the noise level in this classroom is unacceptable. I could hear you all the way down the hall."

"We were doing math," Mr. E. said. "Right, class?"

My friends all nodded.

Mrs. Wright fingered the whistle and I braced myself for an unsqueakably loud noise. Luckily, none came.

"That's funny," she said. "I thought you were playing basketball."

Mr. E. smiled and looked at my classmates. "What were we playing?"

"Mathketball!" my friends all answered.

Mrs. Wright frowned even more, if that's possible. "Perhaps you can do math more quietly in the future," she said. "Of course, I'm sure Mrs. Brisbane will be back tomorrow."

I crossed my paws and hoped that she was right.

Oh, how I hoped that she was right.

Because school with Mr. E. was making me VERY-VERY-VERY *piewhacked*!

(That means "confused.")

HUMPHREY'S DETECTIONARY: It's not easy to solve the mystery of a missing person. Especially if you miss that missing person a lot!

The Case of the Mystifying Mr. E.

After Mrs. Wright left, Mr. E. said, "We've had enough Mathketball for today. But if I'm here again tomorrow, we're going to have a Word War!"

My friends seemed excited about that, but I was worried. Wasn't Mrs. Brisbane coming back tomorrow? Where was she? What was wrong?

I had no clue.

I was ready for a nap, but right away, Mr. E. started another game called "Who's Missing?"

First, he picked Daniel to sit with his back to the classroom. Then, all the other students had to run around and switch places at their tables, except for one. He silently led Forgetful-Phoebe to the cloakroom to hide.

Next, Daniel had to turn back and guess who was missing. It was a lot harder than it sounds, but he guessed Phoebe on the third try. (Which was a good thing, since Mr. E. only gave him three tries!)

The class played the game over and over because everybody wanted a chance to be the guesser. I got drowsy after a while and went into my sleeping hut for a nap. And you know what? No one even noticed that *I* was missing! I know, because I ALWAYS-ALWAYS-ALWAYS wake up when I hear my name.

When I came out again, my classmates were begging Mr. E. to read to them. He smiled and said, "Okay."

He reached into his big bag and pulled out a book.

"No!" Stop-Talking-Sophie said. "We want Sherlock Holmes!"

"It's the red book on the desk," Hurry-Up-Harry said. "Mrs. Brisbane's reading us the story 'The Red-Headed League.'"

Mr. E. made a face. "That's too serious. My book is a lot more fun."

"Sherlock Holmes—please!" Tall-Paul and Small-Paul both said.

Soon, all my friends were saying, "Sherlock Holmes! Sherlock Holmes!"

But Mr. E. sat down and opened his book.

"Can you hear us? We REALLY-REALLY-REALLY want Sherlock Holmes!" I squeaked so hard, my whiskers wiggled and my ears jiggled.

Even Og agreed. "BOING-BOING!"

But Mr. E. went right ahead and read us jokes from his big joke book.

I like jokes a lot, really I do. I especially like this one: *Why are frogs so happy? Because they eat whatever bugs them!*

I thought Og would like that one!

Mr. E.'s jokes were funny. At least in the beginning they were funny.

Like this one: *Where do you put a sick insect? In an ant-bulance!*

My friends laughed hysterically.

I chuckled, too, but after a while, I started worrying about Mrs. Brisbane again. Then I couldn't laugh at all.

Finally, the laughter got quieter and quieter.

Too-Helpful-Holly yawned and raised her hand. "Now could you read from the Sherlock Holmes book?" she asked. "It's a mystery."

Mr. E. chuckled. "Why do you need Sherlock Holmes? *I'm* a Mister E.!"

The mystery about Mister E. was this: When was he going to teach us anything?

〜•〜

Lunchtime came at last and the classroom was quiet again, which was a relief.

Then the door opened and something wonderful happened. Ms. Mac walked in.

Ms. Mac was the substitute teacher who brought me from Pet-O-Rama, my first home (if you can call it that), to Room 26 of Longfellow School. But later, Mrs. Brisbane came back and Ms. Mac left and my heart was broken.

Now Ms. Mac was a full-time teacher at Longfellow School, but in another classroom.

Of course, I love Mrs. Brisbane, too. If I could have one wish come true, it would be that Ms. Mac and Mrs. Brisbane could both be my teachers at the same time!

"Hi." Ms. Mac was smiling. "I'm Morgan McNamara from first grade."

Our substitute teacher shook her hand. "I'm Eddie Edonopolous, but the children call me Mr. E."

Ms. Mac smiled her big, beautiful smile. "I'm sure they like that. I subbed for Mrs. Brisbane last year, and if you need anything, just ask. Have you found her lesson plans?"

"Uh, no. Not yet," he said.

Ms. Mac opened one of Mrs. Brisbane's desk drawers. "She keeps them in here in this binder. Mrs. Brisbane always has very thorough lesson plans."

"Great," Mr. E. said. "I've been getting to know the kids, you know, having a little fun."

"I just heard she might be out for a while," Ms. Mac told him. "She really worries about her students when she's not here."

That was nice to hear because, to squeak the truth, I was really worried about Mrs. Brisbane.

"If you have any questions, I'm right down the hall," Ms. Mac said.

"Thanks," Mr. E. said.

Of course, Ms. Mac wouldn't leave Room 26 without saying hello to Og and me.

She came over to our table by the window. "How's it going, Humphrey, you handsome hamster?" she asked.

No wonder I love Ms. Mac! I scurried over to the side of my cage so I could get a closer look at her.

"It's been a STRANGE-STRANGE-STRANGE day," I replied. "Where is Mrs. Brisbane?"

28

"I know you miss Mrs. Brisbane," she said. Then she turned to Og. "And how's my favorite frog today?"

Og leaped into the water side of his tank and splashed loudly, which made Ms. Mac laugh. I love to hear her laugh.

"I've got to eat," she said, turning back to Mr. E. "Can I show you where the lunchroom is?"

"Sure, thanks," he said, following her out the door.

‿◞◟‿

I rarely leave my cage during the day because it's just too risky. However, this was an emergency. So while we were alone, I jiggled the lock on my cage and scurried over to Og's tank. I'm so lucky to have a lock-that-doesn't-lock. Humans always think it's fastened tight, but I know how to wiggle it open.

"Og," I squeaked. "Something's wrong!"

"BOING-BOING!" he said. Then he dived from the land side of his tank to the water side.

I had to scramble to stay dry. (Hamsters should never get wet.)

Once he stopped splashing, I went back to the tank and said, "Mrs. Brisbane wouldn't miss school unless something was terribly wrong! And Ms. Mac said she might be out for a while. Ms. Mac always tells the truth—right?"

Og splashed frantically again, and again I scrambled for a dry spot.

"Og, if you could splash a little less, I'd appreciate it,"

I told him. "Although I know you are a frog and frogs do splash."

He must have understood, because he stopped.

"Sherlock Holmes always looks for clues," I said. "So keep your ears open, okay?"

I felt terrible as soon as I said it because Og doesn't have any ears (that I can see, anyway).

I glanced up at the clock. I didn't have much time before the class returned from lunch.

"Oh, and by the way, I don't think you're an 'it,'" I said as I headed back to my cage. "And I know you don't think I'm a rat."

"BOING-BOING-BOING!" Og twanged.

I managed to pull the cage door behind me just as my friends returned to their desks.

⌒•⌒

The afternoon went pretty much like the morning. There was no Mathketball, but Mr. E. pulled out three smaller balls from his big sack and juggled them.

Yes, he juggled! It was quite amazing to see him toss the balls into the air and keep them going. Mrs. Brisbane had certainly never done that. It made my brain whirl when I tried to keep my eyes on the balls.

Then Mr. E. let my friends try juggling.

Harry couldn't keep even one ball in the air, but he didn't seem too upset about it.

Next, it was Thomas's turn. "You should see my dad juggle. He can juggle fifteen balls at a time," he said.

Mr. E. looked amazed.

30

"And knives, too. He can juggle knives," Thomas added. "And . . . baseball bats!"

Juggling large, sharp objects sounded downright dangerous.

I heard Rolling-Rosie say, "Give me a break!"

Just-Joey rolled his eyes.

Thomas managed to juggle the balls a few seconds, but then he dropped them and they rolled across the classroom.

"Perhaps your dad can give you some pointers," Mr. E. said.

Phoebe caught the balls on her first try but then dropped them. When Daniel tried, he managed to keep two of the balls going for a few seconds.

It looked like fun, but I couldn't help thinking about Mrs. Brisbane.

She'd be teaching us something interesting about the clouds or the ancient Egyptians or reading something wonderful like Sherlock Holmes.

And here we were, going through an entire afternoon without learning anything except how to juggle!

~·~·~

Near the end of the day, when Mr. E. finally stopped juggling, Helpful-Holly raised her hand.

"It's time to take care of Humphrey and Og," she said. "They need to be fed, and Humphrey needs fresh water. Tomorrow he gets his cage cleaned."

"I don't know how to do those things," Mr. E. said.

Holly explained that the students took turns at the

job. This week it was Phoebe's turn to look after me and Harry's turn to look after Og.

When Harry threw some Froggy Food Sticks into the tank, Og made a huge, splashy leap to get to them.

I could tell my friends were impressed.

Mr. E. was impressed, too. "He's quite a jumper."

"That's nothing," Thomas said. "Once I saw Og leap up out of his tank and land all the way on Mrs. Brisbane's desk!"

Some of my friends laughed.

"That didn't happen," Simon said.

"You're exaggerating," Holly said.

Thomas just shook his head. "I know what I saw," he told them.

I'd seen Og pop the top of his tank a few times, but I'd never seen him leap to Mrs. Brisbane's desk!

Phoebe gave me fresh water, which tasted much better than the old water in my bottle.

"Oh, no!" Phoebe suddenly said. "Mrs. Brisbane always brings fresh veggies for Humphrey."

Yes, she does, and I look forward to them. I always have Nutri-Nibbles and Mighty Mealworms, but there's nothing as crunchy and munchy as fresh veggies. In fact, I hide them in my cheek pouch and in my bedding. But the cage cleaner always finds them and takes them away.

"You don't have any?" Mr. E. asked.

Phoebe looked WORRIED-WORRIED-WORRIED as she shook her head.

"I do!" a voice called out.

Thomas rummaged through his backpack. "I didn't eat my carrot sticks," he said. "Humphrey can have them. I don't like them."

I was extremely grateful to Thomas, though why anyone wouldn't like carrot sticks is a mystery to me.

My friends take very good care of me.

～•～

At the end of the day, Helpful-Holly raised her hand again. "We need our homework assignment," she said.

A lot of the other students tried to shush her, but Holly was determined. "Mrs. Brisbane always gives us homework."

Mr. E. replied that he had a big surprise for the class: the only homework assignment was to bring in a riddle or joke for the next day.

"You don't even have to write it down," he said. Then he tapped his finger on the side of his head. "Just remember it up here."

It was a pretty strange homework assignment. But then, it had been a pretty strange day.

When the bell rang, my friends all looked happy as they left the class.

"Bye, Mr. E.!" Thomas said on his way out of class. "See you tomorrow."

"Bye, Mo-Momas," Mr. E. said. I thought he was mixed up until I remembered the name song.

I heard Hurry-Up-Harry tell Slow-Down-Simon, "Pretty sweet—no homework."

"Mr. E. is a great teacher!" Simon said.

"He's so funny!" Kelsey told Rosie.

After the students had left, Mr. E. sighed a big sigh and said, "That went well." He strolled over to the table by the window where Og and I live. "I think they liked me."

"YES-YES-YES," I shouted. "And they like Mrs. Brisbane, too."

Of course, all he heard was "SQUEAK-SQUEAK-SQUEAK."

Mr. Morales came into the room. "I'm glad I caught you, Ed," he said. "Are you available to teach tomorrow?"

Mr. E. said yes, and then the principal said, "I wasn't able to talk to Mrs. Brisbane, but her husband said her lesson plans are in the desk."

"Yes, I know," Mr. E. said.

"Good!" Mr. Morales said. "I'll see you tomorrow."

The two men shook hands and Mr. Morales left.

When the door closed, Mr. E. chuckled. "That's good news for me."

Then he opened Mrs. Brisbane's desk drawer and took out the binder with the lesson plans in it.

Whew! He was finally thinking about teaching his students. I watched him as he turned the pages.

"Math problems, vocabulary, art project, science—wow, she really packs a lot in," he said aloud.

"YES-YES-YES!" I agreed.

"I don't know about all this," he said. He turned another page. "And that's not going to work."

Og started splashing around in his tank. I was worried, too. After all, these were Mrs. Brisbane's lesson plans. And Mr. E. didn't seem to like them.

Mr. E. closed the binder. "I'm going to have to make these subjects a lot more fun to make this work," he said. "A *lot* more fun."

He was still muttering under his breath when he picked up his big bag and left Room 26.

I had no idea what he was muttering about.

And I still had no idea what had happened to Mrs. Brisbane.

But I had a BAD-BAD-BAD feeling that it wasn't something good.

HUMPHREY'S DETECTIONARY: A detective without any clues is like a classroom without a real teacher!

The Case of the Curious Clues

Once the room was quiet, I hopped on my wheel and spun as fast as my legs would go. Spinning helps me think, and I had a lot of thinking to do.

I waited and waited for Aldo to come in and clean. Maybe he would tell me what had happened.

Suddenly, I was blinded and Aldo's voice boomed, "Hey, buddies, how's it going?"

"Things are unsqueakably bad!" I told him as my eyes adjusted to the lights.

Aldo wheeled his cleaning cart into Room 26 and toward our table. "I guess you heard about Mrs. Brisbane," he said, leaning down to look in my cage.

"WHAT-WHAT-WHAT happened?" I screeched.

Aldo shook his head. "Who'd have thought? I don't have to tell you what I think of Mrs. Brisbane. She inspired me to want to be a teacher."

Aldo goes to school in the daytime so he can teach school someday. He's an excellent cleaner, but I think he'll be a great teacher, too.

"Like I said to Maria, boy, you never know what's going to happen next."

Maria was Aldo's wife and a special human to me.

"I don't even know what happened today," I tried to tell him.

"I know, I know," he said. "You miss her."

Then Aldo went to work. Usually, I love to watch him clean. He sweeps and swoops. He dusts and polishes. He hums and sings and sometimes does a dance.

But he was quieter that night. Oh, he did get the room very clean, but there was no humming, singing or dancing. Every once in a while he'd stop, shake and mumble, "What a thing to happen," or, "You just never know."

I certainly didn't know what was going on and I wished someone would tell me.

When he was finished, Aldo took out a sandwich and his thermos of coffee and sat in front of Og and me. He usually had his dinner break with us, and he always remembered to bring me veggies.

"Here you go, Humphrey, old pal," he said as he pushed a sweet, crunchy celery stick into my cage.

"THANKS-THANKS-THANKS," I squeaked.

Then he dropped a fishy frog stick into Og's tank. My neighbor splashed happily.

"Hey, I was thinking about that Sherlock Holmes book," Aldo said. "I think I'm going to read that story about the redhead again."

"Read it now!" I begged him. "Please!"

But Aldo just ate and packed up his cleaning supplies and wheeled his cart out of Room 26.

"You two have a good night," he said as he switched off the lights.

I was disappointed to see him go. It might be a long time before I had the chance to hear the end of that story.

But after I thought about it some more, I decided to take things into my own paws.

When I saw the lights of Aldo's car leave the parking lot near my window, I jiggled the lock-that-doesn't-lock and opened my cage.

First, I needed to talk to Og. "I was thinking, if we knew how Sherlock Holmes solved a mystery, maybe we could solve our mystery," I squeaked.

"BOING-BOING?" Og twanged.

"I mean, the mystery of what happened to Mrs. Brisbane," I explained patiently.

I try hard to be patient with Og because frogs don't always think like hamsters. I guess they wouldn't, since we're different species.

"Don't worry, Og," I said. "I have a Plan."

Aldo had very kindly left the blinds open so the streetlight outside lit up the room inside.

I moved to the edge of the table and grabbed on to the leg. Taking a deep breath, I glided down. I've done it many times before. It's thrilling and slightly scary and definitely dangerous. Once I hit the floor, I scurried over to Mrs. Brisbane's desk.

That desk is extremely tall from a hamster's-eye view.

I had another lucky break. Mrs. Brisbane's chair was

pushed close to the drawers of her desk, so getting to the big red book on top wouldn't be too difficult. I stood on my tippy toes and reached up to grab the bar between the chair legs. I used every ounce of strength I could gather to pull myself up. Then I grabbed the next-highest bar and—*OOOF*—pulled myself up again.

All the exercise I get spinning my wheel and rolling in my hamster ball has made me a super-strong hamster! (Those veggies help, too.)

Next I grabbed on to the arm of the chair and inched my way up to the seat.

Whew! I was so tired, my whiskers were wilting, but I was only halfway to my goal!

Og sent me some encouraging BOING-BOINGs.

I rested for a few seconds, then reached up again, grabbed the edge of the desk, pulled myself UP-UP-UP and threw myself onto the desktop. Whew!

Og splashed excitedly.

After I caught my breath, I hurried over to the big book with the thick red cover.

Along the side, in big black letters it read: *The Adventures of Sherlock Holmes*.

I felt a little shiver as I looked at the picture of the great man with his deerstalker hat.

"BOING-BOING-BOING!" Og called impatiently.

"Okay, okay, I'm going to open the book," I squeaked back. "We'll find out how to be detectives soon!"

I reached up to touch the edge of the top cover.

"Umph!" I pushed hard with both paws.

Nothing happened.

I pushed again—harder.

Nothing happened. *Again!*

"It's very heavy, Og!" I squeaked, but I was so out of breath, I'm not sure he could hear me. "I wish there weren't quite so many stories about Sherlock Holmes!"

When I failed to budge the cover the third time, I decided to try something else. I looked around the desk-top and saw a pencil. Maybe I could use that to push the cover open.

I rolled it over to the book, propped it up under the cover and gave it a mighty push.

It pushed right back, I guess, and I fell backward. The pencil rolled off the edge of the desk. (I hate to think what would have happened if *I'd* rolled off the edge.)

As I tried to catch my breath, I heard Og splashing wildly.

"BOING-BOING-BOING-BOING-BOING!"

"I'm all right, Og," I called to him. "But I can't get the book open."

I'm not one to give up easily, but I was exhausted and I knew it wouldn't be long before school began. It hadn't been a successful night, but it would be even worse if I got caught outside my cage.

So I slid down the side of the desk (much faster than when I'd climbed up). I raced across the floor and grabbed on to the long cord that hangs down from the blinds.

Then came that hard part where I had to swing back

and forth, higher and higher, until I was level with the top of the table. I let go and slid across the table, past Og's tank, right up to the door of my cage.

"I made it, Og!" I told my friend.

"BOING!" He sounded relieved.

I was planning on a nice doze when I got back in my cage. But when I closed my eyes and was about to drift off, I remembered Mrs. Brisbane saying, "A clue is information that helps you solve a mystery. Sherlock Holmes is very good at finding clues."

I didn't just remember her words; I could hear them in my tiny ears.

I jumped up and raced to the side of my cage. "Og! Mrs. Brisbane said to look for clues. Let's see if we have any clues to what happened to her."

I grabbed the tiny notebook Ms. Mac gave me long ago and the teeny pencil that goes with it. I keep it well hidden behind the mirror in my cage.

I opened it and began to write.

Clue 1: Mrs. Brisbane didn't plan to be absent. The day before, she said, "See you in the morning."
Clue 2: Mr. Morales didn't know Mrs. Brisbane would be absent. He said they were trying to reach her. That's why he took over the class until they could get a substitute. Whatever happened was unexpected.
Clue 3: Mrs. Wright said she was sure Mrs. Brisbane would be back tomorrow. But later in the day, Ms. Mac and

Mr. Morales both said she might be out for a while.
So the story changed as the day went on.
Clue 4: Aldo seems worried that something happened to
Mrs. Brisbane. And that makes me unsqueakably
worried, too.

My paw started shaking, so I quit writing.

I wondered if Sherlock Holmes was ever as worried as I was that morning.

Miss Swift unlocked the door to let Mr. E. in. He had on a button with a big smiley face, and his big cloth bag looked even fuller than it had the day before.

Once my fellow classmates arrived, Mr. Morales came in. His tie for the day had little red birds on it.

"Class, your families were all notified last night about Mrs. Brisbane," he said. "As you know, Mr. E. will be taking over."

My friends all looked perfectly happy, but I was not!

Principal Morales might have told all the families about Mrs. Brisbane last night, but nobody told me! Would Mr. E. be taking over just for now . . . or would it be forever?

I was so worried, I could hardly concentrate on our classwork that morning. Not that there was much. Mr. E. started off the day by having all the students share their jokes. That was their homework, after all.

My friends' jokes were pretty funny.

Hurry-Up-Harry had a good one. "Why does a stork

stand on one leg?" he asked. His answer: "Because if it raised both legs, it would fall down."

And Rolling-Rosie made everyone groan when she asked, "What's brown and sticky? A stick!"

Phoebe forgot to bring a joke. "But I know one," she said. "What do you say to a crying whale? Quit your blubbering!"

Everyone seemed so happy, I began to think maybe nothing bad had happened to Mrs. Brisbane at all. Maybe she'd just gone on vacation.

But then I remembered her saying, "See you in the morning."

I've learned enough about humans to know that they don't leave on vacations without planning ahead.

Especially a human like Mrs. Brisbane.

HUMPHREY'S DETECTIONARY: Clues can make you WORRY-WORRY-WORRY.

The Case of the Afternoon Accident

The rest of the morning was a blur.

First, Mr. E. reached in his sack and pulled out a big rolled-up map. He tacked it on the bulletin board and taught my friends a game called Map Attack. I couldn't really see what was going on because they stood in front of the map and blocked my view. It got very noisy, and the rest of the class seemed to have fun.

Next came Animal Addition. This time, Mr. E. pulled out finger puppets in different animal shapes and the class played some kind of adding and subtracting game. I don't know why they needed *fake* animals when there were two perfectly good *real* animals in the room. But nobody seemed to notice Og and me.

My classmates enjoyed the game, but I thought the problems were a little easy for them. Especially for Small-Paul, who is a math whiz.

Then right after lunch, something odd happened.

The door opened and my friends all streamed in, talking and giggling as usual.

But when they were all in their seats, I noticed that

one chair was empty. Were they playing the game they'd played yesterday?

"Who's missing?" I squeaked loudly.

I guess I didn't squeak loudly enough.

Luckily, Helpful-Holly also noticed that Harry was missing.

"Excuse me, Mr. E.?" she said.

"Yes, Holly?" he asked.

She pointed at Harry's empty chair. "Harry didn't come back from lunch."

Mr. E. looked at the empty chair and scratched his head. "Oh," he said. "Does anyone know where he is?"

I didn't have any idea, and neither did any of my friends.

Holly's hand shot up. "I'll go look for him," she said.

"I'm sure he'll turn up in a minute," Mr. E. said.

I don't think Mrs. Brisbane would ever say that. She'd worked hard since the beginning of school to help Hurry-Up-Harry learn to be on time.

Mrs. Brisbane spends a lot of time thinking up ways to help her students. Or at least she *did*.

I spent a lot of time thinking up ways to help Mrs. Brisbane. But how could I help her if she wasn't here?

Mr. E. was trying to tell my friends how to play Word War when the door opened and Harry strolled in.

"Welcome back," Mr. E. said. "Glad you can join us."

"Thanks," Harry said.

That was it! Did Mr. E. think it was fine for Harry to come to class whenever he felt like it?

The game began when Mr. E. wrote a word on the board. Then two students ran up and made a list of new words by adding letters to the beginning or end. They started with *ate* and wrote *mate* and *hate,* then *hated, late, later,* and *slate.*

Whoever came up with the most words won that round. I could tell my friends enjoyed being able to run in the classroom.

They got louder and louder as they cheered each other on as the game got more and more exciting.

Then Mr. E. wrote another word on the board: *eat.*

"I've got it!" Slow-Down-Simon shouted as he raced to the board.

"I know!" Be-Careful-Kelsey said as she ran up to the board.

Simon didn't slow down.

Kelsey forgot to be careful.

The two of them rammed right into each other.

"Ow!" Simon yelled, holding the side of his head.

"Ow!" Kelsey shouted, clapping her hand over her eye.

Kelsey cried a little and Simon kept saying, "Ow! Owww!"

How many times had Mrs. Brisbane tried to think of ways to slow down Simon?

How many times had Mrs. Brisbane encouraged Kelsey to think before doing things? And now that Mrs. Brisbane was gone, look what had happened!

Mr. E. decided to send them to the nurse's office.

"I could go with them," Holly volunteered.

"I think they can manage on their own," Mr. E. told her.

That was the end of Word War, thank goodness.

"What next?" Mr. E. said.

Helpful-Holly raised her hand. "It's time to look after Humphrey and Og," she said.

"Oh, right," Mr. E. said.

Then Holly said, "Humphrey needs his veggies."

"Did anybody bring veggies for the hamster?" Mr. E. asked the class.

The hamster. As if I didn't even have a name.

"Oh, no!" Phoebe exclaimed. "I forgot. Sorry, Humphrey."

I might have felt discouraged, except for the fact that six hands went up in the air. A lot of my friends had remembered to bring me a treat.

Just-Joey offered a piece of lettuce. Tall-Paul brought me a blueberry. Small-Paul brought sunflower seeds—my favorite. Rolling-Rosie had some yummy celery, and Holly offered a tiny bit of broccoli. Thomas gave me his carrot sticks again (which isn't really a good thing because he should eat his veggies every day).

There were so many hamster-licious things to eat, I hid some of them in my cheek pouch and the rest in my bedding.

It's always nice to save a little something for the future.

I was still busily nibbling when Simon and Kelsey came back.

Simon was holding an ice pack on the side of his head. Kelsey held an ice pack on her eye.

"Everything all right now?" Mr. E. asked.

They both nodded and took their seats.

"I think it's story time," Mr. E. said.

My ears twitched when he said that. Was he finally going to read the rest of that Sherlock Holmes story from the big red book?

My friends were on the edges of their chairs as well.

Mr. E. reached in his sack and pulled out a piece of paper, which didn't look anything like a book.

"Let's write our own silly stories," he said.

I sighed. Was I ever going to hear the rest of "The Red-Headed League" and learn how a real detective works?

Mr. E. then asked the class to supply different words: nouns, verbs, words that describe things—oh, I didn't know there were so many different words. He wrote each of them on the piece of paper. Then he made up a silly story using all those words.

The story made no sense at all, but my friends liked it.

The door suddenly burst open and standing there was Mrs. Wright. Her fingers were on her whistle, which made me nervous.

Luckily, she didn't blow it.

In one hand, Mrs. Wright held a clipboard.

"It's Mrs. Wright!" Mr. E. said. "Right?"

"Mr. Ednopop . . . Ednolopopolopolis," Mrs. Wright said. "I'm co-chairperson of the School Safety Committee. I understand there've been injuries in the classroom."

"A little accident," he said. "Kids will be kids."

Mrs. Wright shoved the clipboard toward him. "You will have to fill out an accident report. Their parents will be notified."

"It was just an accident," Mr. E. said.

"There were injuries on school property," she said. "A report must be filed."

Mrs. Wright took a few more steps into the classroom and looked around. "I also had a report of a student wandering the halls after the lunch bell rang. Was that one of yours?" she asked.

"I don't know," Mr. E. said. "Was it?"

"The hallways should be empty after the bell rings," Mrs. Wright said. "I've put a copy of the *rules* under the accident report."

She fingered that silver whistle around her neck. "The report is due in the morning."

I was REALLY-REALLY-REALLY worried that she was about to blow the whistle.

Instead, she turned and walked out the door.

I was glad to see her go. But I was also glad to see that someone was concerned about my classmates besides Og and me!

In the afternoon, I dozed through some other kind of game, but I woke up when I heard Mr. Morales's voice.

It's always important to listen to what the principal has to say. I darted out of my sleeping hut and saw him in front of the class, holding a piece of paper.

"Class, I just received a note from Mrs. Brisbane that she wanted me to share with you all," he said.

"Did you hear that, Og?" I squeaked at the top of my lungs. "A note from Mrs. Brisbane!"

Og splashed wildly, so I guess he heard.

"The note says, 'Dear class, I miss you all and I miss Longfellow School. I miss being home, too. But the good news is that they say I'll be up on my feet and dancing before long! It's funny to think that this all came about because of Humphrey. Please listen to Mr. E. and make me proud of you. Your teacher, Mrs. Brisbane.'"

This all came about because of Humphrey.

Was it really my fault that Mrs. Brisbane was gone?

If she's going to be up on her feet, she must be sitting. But where *is* she?

Why would she leave her class to go dancing? I'd never seen her dance before.

I wasn't just *piewhacked*. I was super-duper *piewhacked*.

After Mr. Morales left, Holly's hand shot up. "Mr. E., where is Humphrey going this weekend?"

"I give up," Mr. E. answered. "Where is he going?"

Holly explained how I go home with a different student each weekend.

"Okay," Mr. E. said. "So who wants to take Humphrey home?"

Every single student raised a hand. Every one!

"Mr. E.!" Holly said. "You have to get written permission from the parents."

Sometimes, I think Holly will grow up to be just like Mrs. Wright. That's not a bad thing, unless she also gets a whistle.

Just then the bell rang, ending the school day.

Some of the students rushed out to catch the school bus. Others crowded around Mr. E., begging to take me home.

"Whoa!" he said. "Calm down. I'm sure Humphrey will be fine on his own this weekend."

Sorry, but I would *not* be fine without tasty treats and clean water and a poo cleanup!

A red-haired woman hurried into the classroom looking worried. She saw Kelsey with the ice pack on her eye and gave her a hug.

It didn't take Sherlock Holmes to figure out that she was Kelsey's mom.

"Are you okay?" she asked, moving the ice pack. "The nurse called."

"Yes," Kelsey said. "Sort of."

"Wow, you're going to have a black eye," her mom said.

"Mom, could we bring Humphrey home for the weekend?" Kelsey asked.

I rushed to the front of my cage to hear what Mrs. Kirkpatrick had to say.

"Humphrey? Oh, little Humphrey! Well, sure. Why not? He'll help take your mind off your eye," she replied.

Mr. E. came over and introduced himself and said he'd be very grateful if she'd take me home. "I think we need some kind of written permission," he said.

"In the middle drawer!" I shrieked. "That's where she keeps the forms."

Mr. E. didn't understand, of course, but Mrs. Kirkpatrick just wrote on a plain piece of paper, and before I knew it, Kelsey was carrying my cage out of Room 26.

"Sorry, Og! I mean, bye! I mean, have a nice weekend!" I shouted.

"BOING-BOING!" he said. It was a slightly sad sound.

I always feel guilty when I go away for the weekend and leave Og behind.

But that Friday, I felt absolutely rotten. After a few days without Mrs. Brisbane, he would probably be extra lonely this weekend.

HUMPHREY'S DETECTIONARY: A mystery: why are some people, even teachers, pawsitively clueless about how to care for a hamster?

The Case of the Baffling Ballerina

I n the car, Mrs. Kirkpatrick wanted to hear about how Simon and Kelsey bumped heads.

But Kelsey just wanted to talk about me!

"I can't believe it," she said. "I've wanted to bring Humphrey home since the first day of school."

That made me feel very nice. But thinking about what Mrs. Brisbane said still made me feel not-so-nice.

This all came about because of Humphrey.

What on earth had I done to send Mrs. Brisbane away?

And how could I undo it?

Kelsey's house was white, with bright orange shutters around the windows that reminded me of Kelsey's hair—and her mom's.

Her big brother, Kevin, was already home from school. He was very tall, and his hair was darker than Kelsey's.

"What's that?" he said, pointing at me.

"Humphrey!" Kelsey answered. "He's our classroom hamster."

"Oh," Kevin answered. "Mom, what's there to eat? I'm so hungry, I could eat anything in sight."

I was glad I'd hidden all those yummy treats in my cheek pouch and bedding. I like to share, but I'm never quite sure when I'll be fed again.

Kevin and his mom went to the kitchen while Kelsey took my cage to her room.

"Humphrey, you're the cutest hamster I ever saw," she told me.

"Thanks," I squeaked. "And you're one of the nicest girls . . ."

Before I could finish my sentence, I looked at Kelsey. She was nice, but the skin around one of her eyes had turned a bright shade of purple with streaks of green and black.

"Eeek!" I squeaked.

Luckily, Kelsey just giggled. That was one time I was happy a human couldn't understand my squeak. I would never want to hurt a friend's feelings.

Kelsey made sure that everything in my cage was in order. Then her mom came in to check on us.

"Oh, Kelsey! Look at your eye!" her mom said. "I'm afraid it will look a lot worse before it goes away."

Kelsey raced to the mirror and looked at herself.

Oddly enough, she smiled. "I'll probably be the only girl at Longfellow School with a black eye," she said. "Probably the only person!"

Kelsey's mom bit her lip and looked at the eye more

closely. "I guess I don't need to take you to the doctor," she said. "The nurse said it was fine."

Kelsey assured her mom that she could see all right.

"I hope you can go to your ballet lesson tomorrow," Kelsey's mom said. "I'd hate for you to miss the very first one."

At the mention of the word *ballet,* Kelsey suddenly looked unsqueakably unhappy. She reached up and touched her purple eye. "It does hurt a little," she said.

Mrs. Kirkpatrick shook her head. "Poor Kelsey. Tell me again how it happened. That boy, Simon, ran into you?"

Kelsey nodded, but there was more to the story than that, and I knew it.

"You ran into each other!" I squeaked.

"And you were just standing there?" Kelsey's mom asked.

Kelsey squinched up her face and thought for a bit. "No. I was running up to the board to answer a question. We both were running up to the board."

"Ah," Mrs. Kirkpatrick said. "So you bumped into each other."

"YES-YES-YES!" I squeaked.

"I think I'll call Simon's mother to see how he is," Kelsey's mom said.

"He's fine, Mom," Kelsey said, rolling her eyes. "It's no big deal."

But Kelsey's mom had already left the room.

A little while later, Kevin wandered into Kelsey's room. He was eating a large (and yummy-looking) sandwich. "What's up with your eye?" he asked.

"A boy ran into me," Kelsey said.

Kevin stared at her eye. "Wow, that's going to be an amazing shiner, Clumsy. I mean Kelsey."

"How rude!" I squeaked loudly.

Clumsy! Kelsey wasn't always careful, but I didn't think she was clumsy!

And what on earth was a "shiner"? Another mystery word!

"Birdbrain," Kelsey muttered.

Kevin just chuckled and wandered out again. I was glad he was gone.

Once we were alone, Kelsey flopped down on the bed. "That's what I am, Humphrey. Clumsy Kelsey, like Kevin said."

I climbed up the side of my cage and looked right at Kelsey. "That's the silliest thing I ever heard," I told her.

"I am," Kelsey said. "I'm always running into things and getting bumped and bruised."

"Because you aren't careful," I explained. "That's what Mrs. Brisbane says. You need to take your time."

"Mom thinks ballet will make me graceful," she said. "But I think it will just make me more clumsy."

I knew ballet was some kind of dancing. In her note, Mrs. Brisbane said she was going to be dancing soon.

Maybe she was learning ballet. Did she think it would make her more graceful?

"What's so great about twirling around on your toes?" she asked.

I thought about it. Twirling was kind of like spinning on my wheel, which is something I LIKE-LIKE-LIKE to do. And I use my toes for all kinds of things, from climbing on my cage to grooming myself.

"Sounds pawsitively great!" I said.

Kelsey got up off the bed, looked in the mirror and smiled. "It's a great shiner," she said. "But whoever heard of a ballerina with a black eye?"

"I don't know," I squeaked. "I've never actually seen a ballerina."

Kelsey walked over to her dresser and picked up a pink box. "Here, Humphrey. I'll show you," she said.

Sometimes I wonder if humans really *can* understand me.

After setting the box next to my cage, Kelsey opened the lid and I saw an amazing thing. There was a tiny dancer—smaller than me—in front of a small mirror. Tinkly music began to play as the ballerina twirled around.

The ballerina was all in pink, with a short pink skirt, and she danced right up on her tippy toes. I was spellbound as I watched her go ROUND-ROUND-ROUND again and again.

"See, that's a ballerina," Kelsey said. "She never trips and falls. She never gets a black eye."

I was disappointed when she suddenly slammed down the lid of the box. The ballerina disappeared from view and the music stopped playing.

"I could never be graceful like her," Kelsey said. "Watch."

Kelsey started spinning around the room. I have to admit, she didn't exactly look like the twirling ballerina. While the tiny dancer twirled in one place, Kelsey lurched around wildly until I was afraid she was going to stumble right into my cage.

She didn't. Instead, she wobbled and fell backward, landing on her tail. (Well, the place where humans would have a tail, if humans had tails.)

"Ouch!" she said.

"Eeek!" I squeaked.

Just then, Simon raced into the room. His mom and Kelsey's mom were right behind him.

"Hi, Kelsey," he said. "My mom wanted to see your eye."

"Kelsey, what are you doing on the floor?" Mrs. Kirkpatrick asked.

Kelsey got up and rubbed her rear end. "Practicing ballet," she said.

Simon walked up to Kelsey and looked closely at her eye. "Wow, that's amazing," he said.

"Does it hurt?" Mrs. Morgenstern asked.

"Not really," Kelsey answered. She pointed at the side of Simon's head. "Hey, you've got a bump."

Simon rubbed his head. "Gee, I'd rather have a shiner."

So . . . a shiner must be a bruised eye!

He turned and saw me. "Hi, Humphrey! Look at my bump."

"Eeek!" I squeaked again. But Simon didn't seem to mind.

"We thought if we all went out for ice cream, you two might forget your injuries for a while," Mrs. Kirkpatrick said.

Kelsey and Simon seemed happy and didn't even remember to say good-bye to me when they all left the room.

⌣·⌣·⌣

When I was alone, I thought about the twirling ballerina.

I can spin on my hamster wheel or in my hamster ball, but twirling looked like fun.

I stood up and tried to twirl, but I tumbled head over toes instead. Somersaults are fun . . . unless you aren't planning on one.

I got up and tried again. This time I manage to twirl around once.

But something was missing: the music!

I knew that it would take my friends a while to get ice cream, so I jiggled my lock-that-doesn't-lock and pushed on it. Once I was out of my cage, I hurried over to the pink box.

I could barely reach the lid, and the first time I pushed, the lid popped up and crashed right back down. But even standing on my tippy toes, I wasn't tall enough to open it.

However, I don't give up easily. So I scurried over to the side of the box near the hinge. And finally, I pushed with all my might and the lid swung open. Phew, that lid was heavy!

The music began to play, and I raced to the front of the box to watch the pretty little ballerina go round and round.

Kelsey was right. The ballerina was a graceful dancer. I watched her whirl and twirl until I felt a little dizzy.

Then, I raised myself up and tried twirling again. I stood UP-UP-UP on my toes and spun myself around in a circle. Then I made another circle. And another. I was twirling and not falling over!

I wished Kelsey could see me. If a furry little hamster could learn to twirl around gracefully, I knew she could, too!

Although I was unhappy about Mrs. Brisbane leaving Room 26, I hoped she would enjoy dancing as much as I was.

My twirling was interrupted by a loud bang and footsteps. Kelsey and Simon were back!

I raced back to my cage and pulled the door behind me. The ballerina was still dancing and the music was playing.

"Humphrey! We brought you a strawberry," Kelsey shouted as she raced into the room.

Simon was right behind her. "Where's the music coming from?" he asked.

"My music box," Kelsey said. "That's funny. It was closed when I left."

Simon laughed. "Maybe Humphrey opened it."

That made Kelsey laugh. "Sure, it was Humphrey."

With the music still going, it was my chance to show

Kelsey that anybody could learn to twirl . . . even a hamster!

I got up on my toes and spun around again and again.

"Look! Humphrey's dancing!" Simon pointed at me.

Kelsey leaned down to watch. "He makes it look easy," she said.

They giggled, of course. The music was getting slower and slower. So was I.

"Can you make it go again?" Simon asked.

Kelsey closed the lid and opened it again. The music was back to speed and the ballerina was spinning.

"Let's do a Humphrey dance," Simon said. He started twirling around the room and laughing.

Kelsey chuckled and started twirling again, too.

"The trick is to pick one place to look," Simon said. "Each time you spin around, look at that spot."

He was a pretty good twirler.

"Hey, it works," Kelsey admitted.

She wasn't staggering. She wasn't stumbling. She was just spinning.

The music slowed down again and we all stopped dancing.

"That reminds me. I have to start ballet lessons to-morrow," Kelsey said. "I don't see how I'll ever dance on my toes."

"Ah, my sister takes ballet. You don't start out on your toes. You start out with simple stuff," he said.

Slow-Down-Simon's sister was Stop-Giggling-Gail. She'd been in Mrs. Brisbane's class last year. I knew she was a great laugher, but I didn't know she took ballet lessons, too!

"Really?" Kelsey said.

"Really," Simon said.

"Let's watch Humphrey dance again," he said.

So I DANCED-DANCED-DANCED some more until finally, it was time for Simon to go home.

⌣·⌣

Before she went to bed that night, Kelsey watched the music box ballerina again for a while.

"It would be nice to have a pretty pink tutu like that," she said. "Maybe I'll like ballet after all."

Tutu? I was *piewhacked* until I realized she was talking about the dress.

Well, I liked ballet, but there was no way *I* was going to wear a pink tutu—ever!

I guess Kelsey read my mind, because she said, "Of course, boy ballet dancers don't dress like that. They wear tights. They don't dance up on their toes, but they lift the girl dancers way up in the air."

Whew! I was relieved to learn that.

Kelsey slept well that night. And even though I'm usually awake for some of the night, I slept unsqueakably well, too.

I guess it was all that twirling.

⌣·⌣

On Saturday afternoon, Kelsey left for her dance class. I crossed my toes and hoped that she would enjoy her first lesson.

While she was gone, I couldn't resist leaving my cage to watch the tiny ballerina dance again. I made sure I was back in my cage long before Kelsey got back.

"Humphrey, Humphrey!" she shouted as she raced into the room. "Wait until I show you!"

She stood in front of my cage and noticed that the music box was open.

"I closed that before I left," she said. "Maybe there's something wrong with the lid."

I didn't squeak one word.

"Anyway, I want to show you what I learned at ballet class," she said.

"GOOD-GOOD-GOOD," I replied.

She pointed at her shiny pink shoes. "These are my ballet slippers," she said.

Next she showed me five positions for the feet. And then she did some very graceful dipping moves.

"It was so much fun, Humphrey! And I can be graceful. I just have to pay attention to what I'm doing. That's what our teacher said," Kelsey explained. "At the end of the class, we got to dance around the room with scarves. It was beautiful."

◦◦◦

The next day, Kelsey's eye was a rainbow of colors. But it didn't seem to bother her. She spent a long time practicing the five positions.

I practiced, too, but I guess a hamster's feet work a little differently than human feet. The first three positions weren't too bad, but the fourth and fifth were . . .

well, let's just say, I'm going to have to practice a whole lot more.

And pay attention to what I'm doing.

HUMPHREY'S DETECTIONARY: I don't know if Sherlock Holmes ever tried ballet dancing, but he should have because it's FUN-FUN-FUN.

The Case of the Colorful Cards

When Kelsey brought me back on Monday morning, everybody rushed over.

"Whew! That's some black eye!" Rosie exclaimed.

Actually, it was purple and gray with pink and green stripes, but I didn't correct her.

"How's it feel?" Mr. E. asked her.

"Fine," Kelsey said.

She set my cage on the table in front of the window and walked very carefully—and gracefully—back to her desk.

"BOING-BOING!" Og greeted me cheerily.

Then Simon came in and everybody wanted to touch the bump on his head.

"Okay," he told Small-Paul. "But not too hard."

"That's nothing," Thomas said, holding the back of his head. "I hit my head and had to get ninety-five stitches here."

"That explains a lot," Just-Joey muttered as he walked by.

Tall-Paul bent down and looked at Thomas's head. "Funny, there's no scar."

"Ninety-five?" Simon asked. I'm pretty sure he didn't believe Thomas. "Are you sure?"

"If you got ninety-five stitches in your head, you'd be sure," Thomas said.

My friends all went to their seats, and as soon as the bell rang, Helpful-Holly raised her hand.

"Mr. E., we always have a vocabulary test on Monday," she said.

There were lots of groans from the other students and some of them went "Shhh! Shhh!"

"Well, we won't have one this Monday," Mr. E. replied. "Because today we'll have—"

He didn't finish his sentence because just then Mr. Morales walked into the classroom. He was wearing a tie with horses all over it. (I wonder if they make a tie with hamsters all over it?)

"Class, I have another note from Mrs. Brisbane. She says, 'I'm getting stronger every day. Today, I was actually able to put on my slippers. I think of you all every day.'"

Slippers? Kelsey said that's what ballerinas wear. And Mrs. Brisbane had said she'd be dancing soon.

So, just as I thought, Mrs. Brisbane really was learning ballet!

"I have an address for her now," Mr. Morales said. "So I think it would be nice if you'd all make cards and we'll send them off to her."

"Great idea," Mr. E. said. "We'll start on it right away."

After Mr. Morales left, Mr. E. passed out colorful paper. He told my classmates to start writing their messages to Mrs. Brisbane while he gathered up art supplies.

Holly's hand shot up in the air. "They're over there on the shelves. I can show you!"

"No, thanks, Holly. You start writing," Mr. E. replied. "Now be sure to make your card reflect your personality."

"Can I take this home and work on it tonight?" Daniel asked.

"Try to Do-It-Now-Daniel," Mr. E. told him. "If you don't finish, you can take it home."

Soon, all of my classmates were bent over their tables, working.

All except for Joey. He stared at his paper, but he didn't write one word.

I scrambled up to the top of my cage to see if I could read what my other friends were writing, but I couldn't make out the letters from so far away.

I wanted to write to Mrs. Brisbane, too, but I didn't dare take out my notebook in case someone saw it. And as much as I like my friends, my notebook is private. (No one should *ever* read something that's private.)

While my friends wrote, things were clinking and clanging and rattling and rolling around as Mr. E. poked around in the art supply bins. Soon, there was a big mound of markers and boxes of colored pencils and crayons on the desk. I saw more construction paper, brightly colored yarn, scissors, glue, and jars of buttons, beads and glitter.

When Mr. E. told my friends to take what art supplies they needed for their cards, everyone raced forward at once.

"I wanted those markers!" Simon said.

"I got here first," Thomas replied, clutching the markers to his chest.

"Oooh, feathers!" Phoebe said.

Rolling-Rosie rolled toward the desk. "Hey, I need those," she said.

"Ow! Rosie ran over my foot!" Sophie complained.

"Did not!" Rosie said.

My friends never acted like that when Mrs. Brisbane was in the classroom.

I could hardly tell what anyone was saying because there was so much commotion.

Suddenly, my whole body was shaken by the shrill and painful blast of a whistle!

Everyone got quiet then.

I didn't even have to look to know that Mrs. Wright was standing in the doorway.

"What's going on here?" she asked.

"We're making cards for Mrs. Brisbane," the substitute answered.

"What you're making is an uproar," she said. "I could hear you way down the hall. And according to the school policy, you should *not* be able to hear what's going on in a classroom from the hallway."

Mrs. Wright walked into the classroom, and I saw that she wasn't alone. Hurry-Up-Harry was with her.

"I don't suppose you noticed that one of your students was missing," she said.

Harry hung his head and looked extremely unhappy.

"I guess I'm still getting used to all the students," Mr. E. said. "Come on in, Harry. Make a card for Mrs. Brisbane."

Mrs. Wright fingered the whistle hanging down from her neck. I braced myself, just in case she blew it again.

"Mr. Edopopopolous, at Longfellow School, we don't permit our students to roam the halls whenever they want," Mrs. Wright said. "I found Harry staring into the window of Room Fourteen!" She sounded shocked.

"They're building an amazing tower," Harry explained.

"What's amazing is that you weren't in your classroom, like all the other students at school," Mrs. Wright said. "I will have to report Harry to the principal."

"I'll handle this," Mr. E. said.

Mrs. Wright looked surprised. "Really? You'll put in a report?"

Mr. E. nodded. "That's right, Mrs. Wright."

I was surprised—and relieved—when Mrs. Wright and her whistle left the room. But I was sorry that Hurry-Up-Harry was going to get in trouble. He'd gotten in trouble a lot at the beginning of the year for being late. But he'd been so much better . . . until Mr. E. arrived.

"Do I have to go to the office?" Harry asked.

"No, Harry. But this class is just as much fun as Room Fourteen," Mr. E. said. "Come on. Let's make cards! Make them funny and bright with lots of pizzazz!"

Pizzazz? What on earth was *pizzazz*? I'd never heard that word before. I'd never seen it on a vocabulary list, either.

Was it like glitter and beads and glue? Or was it like pizza?

Whatever it was, it was definitely a mystery word that I found very *piewhacking*!

My friends spent the rest of the morning on the cards, working furiously. Feathers flew, scissors snipped, and there was glitter everywhere.

Joey still seemed to be struggling as he stared at his card. Maybe Joey needed help, but Mr. E. didn't seem to notice.

I think Mrs. Brisbane would have noticed.

When the bell for lunch rang, my friends raced out the door while Mr. E. restacked the art supplies.

"Everything okay?" Ms. Mac said as she poked her head in the door.

"Fabulous," Mr. E. said. "Better than I ever expected. Wait . . . I'll walk to the lunchroom with you."

At last, Og and I were alone!

"Og!" I squeaked excitedly.

"BOING!" he twanged.

"The class is a mess without Mrs. Brisbane!" I shouted. "The students are falling back into their bad habits! Harry's late again, and there's too much noise and no vocabulary quiz or Sherlock Holmes!"

Og splashed wildly in the water side of his tank. "BOING-BOING-BOING-BOING!"

I could tell he was almost as upset as I was.

"*And* I want to make Mrs. Brisbane a card!" I said.

"BOING-BOING!"

"*And* I want to find out where she is!" I added.

"BOING-BOING-BOING!"

There was so much to think about.

I wondered if Harry would get back to class on time.

I wondered if Mr. E. would teach us something in the afternoon.

I wondered if Mrs. Brisbane would EVER-EVER-EVER be back!

My fellow students came back after lunch—all except one.

Hurry-Up-Harry wasn't missing, but Forgetful-Phoebe was!

However, she showed up right after the bell rang.

"Sorry, Mr. E.," she said.

"Not a problem," he answered. "Take a seat, because now we're going to play . . . Math Monsters!"

He took his fingers and pulled out the corners of his mouth and the corners of his eyes. He looked pretty creepy, especially when he made a scary laugh, like a witch.

"After all . . . you know what's coming soon!" he continued.

There was a pause and then Thomas shouted, "Halloween!"

Then everyone else started shouting, "Halloween!"

My classmates seemed happy about it. But I remembered last year's Halloween, with creepy smiling pumpkins and ghosts and goblins and monsters. Now it was coming back? Eeek!

❧

After school, Og and I had some visitors.

"Hello," Mr. E. greeted them. "What can I do for you?"

"We were in this class last year," a soft voice said. It was Speak-Up-Sayeh! She was one of my best friends in Room 26 last year. "We came to see Humphrey and Og."

"Be my guest," Mr. E. said, and soon, Og and I were surrounded by familiar, friendly faces.

"Hi, Humphrey Dumpty! Boy, bad news about Mrs. Brisbane!" That was good old A.J.'s loud voice.

"YES-YES-YES!" I agreed.

"Poor Humphrey! Poor Og! You must miss Mrs. Brisbane a lot," said Golden-Miranda. She was such a wonderful friend . . . with a terrible dog. "But I'm sure she misses you, too."

"Hi, Humphrey! Winky says hi!" said Mandy, whose hamster, Winky, was a friend of mine.

It was great to see my old friends. But it was sad, too,

because they reminded me of happy days in Room 26 with Mrs. Brisbane.

My teacher.

Or was she?

HUMPHREY'S DETECTIONARY: It's a mystery to me why humans enjoy a very frightening holiday like Halloween!

The Case of the Mysterious Messages

Mamma mia! What happened here?" Aldo said as he pulled his cleaning cart into the room and looked around.

I looked around, too, and what I saw was almost as scary as Halloween.

The room was a mess. On the floor were scraps of paper, yarn, buttons, beads, markers and crayons. On top of the tables were scissors and overturned glue bottles. And there was glitter glistening on the floor like snow.

"EEEK-EEEK-EEEK!" I squeaked.

"BOING-BOING-BOING!" Og twanged.

Aldo leaned on his broom and shook his head. "I can tell Mrs. Brisbane wasn't here today. She never leaves her room messy at the end of the day."

"That's for sure!" I agreed.

Aldo didn't have much time to talk. He was too busy sweeping and spraying and scrubbing and mopping up the room.

He stopped when he saw the stack of cards. "Oh,

they're making cards for Mrs. Brisbane. Good idea!" he said. "I'd like to send her a card myself."

"Me too!" I squeaked.

"BOING-BOING!" Og agreed.

After the room was in order and the art supplies neatly stacked on Mrs. Brisbane's desk, Aldo took out his lunch and pulled up a chair close to Og's tank and my cage.

When he finished eating, he went over to Mrs. Brisbane's desk, took a piece of paper and wrote something on it. He folded it in half. Then he wrote on a smaller piece of paper and stuck it on top of the folded paper.

"Now the substitute will include my card with the others," Aldo said.

"Can you write one for me?" I squeaked. Aldo usually seems to understand me. But that night, he didn't.

"Well, I've got to run," he said. "I'll be late getting home tonight and I have to study for a test." Then he looked around the room. "But at least the room is clean."

"Yes, Aldo! You did a GREAT job," I told him. I meant it, too. Aldo is VERY-VERY-VERY good at his job.

"Thanks, Humphrey," Aldo said. He wheeled his cart out of the room and turned off the light.

Luckily, a big full moon was making the room nice and bright. It had been a difficult day, but I was feeling brighter myself.

"Og, I think I'll check out those cards," I said after

Aldo's car left the parking lot. "And maybe I'll get more clues about what happened to Mrs. Brisbane."

"BOING-BOING!" Og said. I'm not sure if he thought my idea was good or if he was just excited about his Froggy Food Sticks.

I took my usual path to get to Mrs. Brisbane's desk and had no trouble.

"I made it, Og!" I told my friend, who was splashing around in his tank.

I looked UP-UP-UP. The stack of cards was about six hamsters high. There was a bright yellow card with sparkles near the bottom. It was sticking out a bit from the rest of the pile, so I decided to grab it and pull.

That was a big mistake, because as the card came out of the stack, the whole pile tumbled down around me and *on* me. Luckily, paper doesn't weigh too much. I wasn't hurt—just surprised.

Still, I now had the chance to look at all the cards and possibly gather more clues about Mrs. Brisbane's "disappearance."

The yellow card with sparkles was from Rosie. The front had red hearts and bright buttons. Inside, it said:

Mrs. Brisbane, I miss you the most! Come back and I'll pop a wheelie for you!

Love, Rosie

The last part was in a big red heart. I'm not sure Mrs. Brisbane would be happy to see Rosie "pop a wheelie" for her. That's a trick she can do with her wheelchair, but Mrs. Brisbane made her promise not to do it at school anymore. I guess Rosie just meant she'd be happy to see our teacher back in the classroom.

Then I looked at a blue card. It was from Small-Paul. On the front was a drawing of a rocket. Inside, it said:

I hope you'll be launched back into Room 26 soon. I miss you!

Paul F.

"Eeek!" I squeaked. Had Mrs. Brisbane been launched into outer space?

Next, I looked at one that was bright pink. It had lots of fancy writing on the outside and the inside:

Dear Mrs. B.,
When you come back to Room 26, I promise to help you all the time. You don't have to worry about anything, because I'll be here for you now and forever! If you ever need something, please call on me.
Your TRUE friend for all time,
Holly

Thomas's card was covered with red, white and blue yarn. It read:

You are the best teacher in the universe!

Thomas

Sometimes Thomas exaggerates, but this time, I thought he was right. But I was shocked when I read what he wrote at the bottom:

PS I am the best juggler in the class. I can juggle for hours without dropping a ball, just like my dad!

That just wasn't true. Why did a nice boy like Thomas make up things like that?

The next card was white with fancy purple letters. It said:

Sometimes I forget things, but I never forget all the nice things you do for us.

Come back soon!
Love, Phoebe

I felt a little pang for Phoebe. She was forgetful, but she was also extremely nice.

Kelsey's card had a drawing of a ballet dancer on it. Inside, it said:

Hope you'll be up on your toes soon!

From Kelsey

There was a very plain orange card with blue letters. No glitter, no beads, no buttons. It said:

I'm not good at fancy words, but I miss you.

Just Joey

Joey's card was nice and simple. I knew Mrs. Brisbane would like it, because it sounded like him.

"Og, these cards are so nice!" I shouted to my friend. "Our friends did a great job!"

He splashed around in a happy-sounding way.

I read all the cards. The more I read, the more I wished I could make a card for Mrs. Brisbane, too.

I looked over at the art supplies. Markers, crayons, glue and glitter make a very nice-looking card. But I also knew they were dangerous . . . at least to hamsters.

Hamsters like me don't wash our paws in soap and water. In fact, soap and water aren't good for us at all. NO-NO-NO! We groom ourselves using our tongues and paws. So if I got glue or markers on my paws and licked it off, I might get very sick.

Maybe I could add some *pizzazz*. Mr. E. had suggested that. But I looked and looked and couldn't find any jar or bottle or box marked *pizzazz*.

I'd have to make a plain card like Just-Joey's.

I went slowly back to my cage. All the cards were great, but one stuck in my mind.

Kelsey had said she hoped Mrs. Brisbane would be up on her toes soon.

Up on her toes? That sounded like a clue. Was Mrs. Brisbane actually going to be a ballet dancer?

I tried to imagine our teacher, with her short gray hair and her sensible shoes, twirling around like a ballerina. She didn't look like the dancer in Kelsey's music box. But if Mrs. Brisbane wanted to be a ballerina, then that's what she should be. (Even though I think she makes a better teacher.)

I pulled out my little notebook and pencil from behind my mirror.

First, I added a clue to my list:

Clue 5: Mrs. Brisbane may be learning to be a ballet dancer.

I wasn't sure about that, so I added a couple of question marks.

????

Next, I turned the page and thought about what to write to my teacher.

I wanted to say just the right thing. I thought and thought and thought some more. Sometimes it's easier to say something you feel in your heart with a poem. And so I wrote:

Roses are red,
Violets are blue,
Oh, Mrs. Brisbane—
How much I miss you!

I looked it over and liked it, so I signed it:

Humphrey

I read it to Og.
"BOING-BOING-BOING-BOING!" he twanged.
"Oops! Sorry, Og," I replied.
Then I added:

Og, too

"I signed your name, too, Og," I assured my neighbor. (He can't write. At least I don't think he can write. And he doesn't have a notebook. If he did, it would have to be waterproof!)

I tore the page from the notebook, but when I looked at it, it seemed a little too plain.

I didn't know how to make it fancier.

I looked around my cage and dug around in my bedding. All I came up with was a tiny piece of carrot I'd saved and the strawberry Kelsey had brought.

It was the juiciest strawberry I'd ever seen.

"Og, I have a great idea!" I squeaked.

I rubbed my paws all over the strawberry to get them nice and juicy. Then I made little red paw prints around the edge. It looked very nice, if I do say so myself.

And when I was finished, I licked the red juice off my paws. Yummy!

Of course, then I had to take the card over to the desk. I picked up the paper with my teeth, jiggled the lock-that-doesn't-lock and opened the door to my cage.

Og splashed gently in his tank as I passed by.

"Oh!" I said. Of course, as soon as I opened my mouth, the paper dropped to the table.

"Sorry, Og," I said. "I wish you could add your mark, too."

"BOING!" Og answered, splashing.

"Or maybe you can! I'm leaving the card here," I explained. "Then I'll go behind my cage. Splash some water, and then I'll come back for the card."

I left the paper near his tank, scurried away and squeaked, "Now!"

Og splashed and splashed some more.

"Not too much," I said. "You can stop now."

I waited until Og stopped splashing and raced back to the paper.

There were several little water marks on the paper now. I HOPED-HOPED-HOPED Mrs. Brisbane would know that Og had made them.

I picked up the paper with my teeth again and made my second trip of the night down the table leg and back to the desk.

The stack of cards was now a mound of cards. There was no way a small hamster could stack them all up again, so I just pushed my card into the pile. Then I made the long trek back to my cage and closed the door behind me.

Morning light streamed in through the window and I was worn out.

"Good night, Og," I said as I crawled into my sleeping hut. "I mean, good morning."

I guess he was tired, too, because he didn't answer. Not even one "BOING."

Or if he did answer, I couldn't hear him because I was sound asleep.

HUMPHREY'S DETECTIONARY: Finding clues can make you unsqueakably tired!

The Case of the Problem Pupils

I lost my watch," I heard Phoebe whisper to Kelsey before class began the next morning. They were standing right next to my cage and Phoebe looked worried. In fact, I'm pretty sure she had tears in her eyes.

I REALLY-REALLY-REALLY hate to see a human cry.

"Oh, no! Your daisy watch? Where did you lose it?" Kelsey asked.

"If I knew where I lost it, I could find it!" Phoebe answered.

That made sense to me.

"Maybe it's in the lost and found," Kelsey suggested. "You should check it out."

Phoebe rolled her eyes. "No way. You heard what Thomas said about the lost and found!"

"It sounds like a creepy place," Kelsey agreed.

Phoebe nodded. "Besides, I don't want to go to Mrs. Wright's office. She doesn't like me. Anyway, the last place I saw it was in the bathroom, but when I went back there, it was gone. I just feel terrible," she said. "My parents gave me that watch, and Grandma would be disappointed if I lost it."

"I'm sorry," Kelsey said.

"Okay, class. Take out your homework from last night," Mr. E. announced.

I was spinning on my wheel at the time and I was so amazed to hear him say "homework" that I almost fell off!

Mr. E. gave homework? When did that happen?

I guess I must have dozed off during class yesterday.

"Who got the answer?" he asked.

I was surprised again when none of my friends raised a hand.

"Let me write that paragraph on the board so we can all look at it together," Mr. E. said.

I raced to the front of my cage so I could watch as he wrote and wrote and wrote some more. This is what he wrote:

> This is an unusual paragraph. I'm curious how quickly you can find out what is so unusual about it. It looks so plain you would think nothing was wrong with it! In fact, nothing is wrong with it! It is not normal, though. Study it, and think about it, but you still may not find anything odd. But if you work at it a bit, you might find out! Try to do so without any coaching!

The paragraph didn't look unusual to me. Just sentences strung together with no mystery words like *piewhack* or *pizzazz*.

"Did anyone figure it out?" Mr. E. asked.

A few hands went up. Mr. E. called on Rosie.

"I think it's unusual because it has so many exclamation points," she said.

"Good answer," the substitute said. "But there's something even more unusual."

Next, he called on Thomas.

"I think it's unusual because it's so long," he said.

Mr. E. nodded. "It's long. But I've seen paragraphs that are a lot longer."

While all of this was going on, I read that paragraph over and over again.

"I'll give you a hint," Mr. E. said. "Something is missing."

"Eeek!" I squeaked as my friends all stared up at the sentence.

Finally, Small-Paul raised his hand. "There's no letter *e* in it," he said.

"E!" I squeaked. He was right!

"That's correct. Did you know that *e* is the letter that shows up more than any other letter in the English language?"

Mr. E. would know that. I'm sure he liked the letter *e* a lot. But I didn't know it. I think it was the first time I'd actually learned something since he arrived in Room 26!

"So now, why don't you try to write a paragraph without using the letter *e*?" Mr. E. said. "While you do that, I'll get these cards ready to send to Mrs. Brisbane."

My friends all went to work, but I didn't. I was too

busy watching Mr. E. stack up the cards. I wanted to make sure that my tiny card was still with the others. Whew! It was!

Then Mr. E. looked at some of the cards. "Joey? Would you like to work on this card a little more?" he asked. "It doesn't have much pizzazz."

"That's okay," Joey answered. "I don't have much pizzazz either. I like things simple."

"Some buttons? Some yarn? A little glitter and glitz?" Mr. E. asked.

Joey shrugged. "No, I like it the way it is."

This time Mr. E. didn't argue.

But I was excited because now I had some clues to figure out what *pizzazz* really meant!

"Og, *pizzazz* isn't like pizza at all!" I squeaked to my friend. "It's glitter and glitz. It's zing and bling! It's that little something extra," I explained.

"BOING?" Og sounded a little *piewhacked*.

"It's fancy instead of plain," I said. "If you had a very fancy pizza, then I think you'd have a pizza with pizzazz!"

Og leaped into the water side of his tank for a swim. I'm not sure he understood what I said, but at least *I'd* figured out that mystery word.

Now if only I could figure out what had happened to Mrs. Brisbane.

And why Mr. E. was a teacher who didn't really teach.

And where-oh-where Phoebe's watch had gone?

After lunch, Mr. E. gave the class free time. He gave them a *lot* of free time!

Some students read. Some drew pictures. Some of them wrote. Some of them walked around the classroom. Some of them even talked. (Something Mrs. Brisbane would not have allowed. For her, free time meant quiet time.)

Only one of them talked to me: that was Phoebe.

"Humphrey, I brought you a piece of apple," she said. "This time I remembered."

"That's unsqueakably nice of you," I replied. I was very honored that Forgetful-Phoebe had remembered me.

Phoebe leaned down close to my cage so I was almost nose to nose with her.

"But I can't remember what I did with my daisy watch," she said. She looked around to see if anyone was listening. No one was . . . not even Og, who was swimming in the water side of his tank.

"My parents gave it to me before they deployed," she said. "They're both in the military, and I miss them a lot. They weren't supposed to be gone at the same time, but then they had to be."

So that's why Phoebe was living with her grandmother.

"I just have to find it. I wouldn't want my mom and dad to know I lost it," she said.

"YES-YES-YES!" I told her. "You have to try very hard!"

I hoped that, somehow, Phoebe understood me.

Phoebe sighed. "I think about Mom and Dad all the time. I guess that's why I don't remember things very well. Mrs. Brisbane was sending reminders home with me every night and calling my grandma when something important was coming up," she explained. "Mr. E. doesn't do that."

Then she grinned. "Of course, he doesn't give us real homework and tests!"

"I noticed," I told her.

"Would it be okay if I looked in your cage?" Phoebe asked. "I was thinking maybe it fell off while I was cleaning it."

"Of course! Please look," I replied. To squeak the truth, I was sure it wasn't in my cage because I know every hiding place there is. But I thought it was a good idea to look, and it was awfully nice of her to ask first. After all, my cage is my home, and as much as I like humans, I don't want them sticking their hands inside all the time.

Phoebe opened the cage door and poked all around. She was doing such a good job of looking, I was afraid she'd find my notebook hidden behind my mirror.

Luckily, she didn't!

"I guess it's not there," she said at last. "I was wishing that you had found it and saved it for me, Humphrey."

I wished her wish had come true!

After free time, Mr. E. said something that curled my toes and wiggled my whiskers. "Folks, it's almost Halloween. While we have the art supplies out, why don't we decorate the room?"

"Eeek!" I squeaked. All I could think of was the leering orange pumpkin someone put close to my cage last year.

"BOING-BOING! BOING-BOING!" Og sounded as alarmed as I was.

But my friends were happy and excited about Halloween.

"Let's give our decorations some pizzazz! We want the ghastliest ghosts! The goriest goblins! The creepiest creeps! And the weirdest witches!" Mr. E.'s red hair seemed to shine a little brighter.

I felt a shiver . . . and a quiver.

"Let's make it the most haunted Halloween ever," he added.

I just couldn't look. I dashed into my sleeping house. But I didn't sleep a wink.

I couldn't stop thinking about Phoebe. Finally, I understood why she was so forgetful. But I didn't have a clue about how to help her.

Also, there were some eerie sounds going on in the classroom.

I heard a ghostly "Oooooo." Then a ghastly laugh . . . like a witch. And a fur-raising howl. Halloween was turning into Howl-a-ween!

I finally had to take a peek outside. Luckily, I didn't see any ghosts or goblins—just my friends drawing, coloring, cutting paper.

So I went back into my sleeping house again. And this time, I took a nap.

~•~

Later in the afternoon, Mr. E. announced that he had a letter from Mrs. Brisbane! I dashed out of my sleeping hut and climbed up high in my cage so I could see and hear everything.

"Pay attention now, Og," I told my froggy friend. "There may be clues."

Og hopped up on a rock and was very quiet.

"Dear class, I hope you are all doing well," Mr. E. read. "I miss you all, but everyone here is very nice and they've got me on my feet. My days are a whirl and they say I'm performing very well. Please be kind to your substitute teacher and to one another. Fondly, Mrs. Brisbane."

My friends all applauded when Mr. E. was finished.

"Did you hear that?" I asked Og. "She *must* be learning to dance. She said she's performing and she's up on her feet."

Og didn't know anything about ballet, and it was hard to explain to him.

~•~

After school, when the classroom was empty except for Og and me, I took out my notebook and looked at my list of clues. I took my little pencil and added two more:

Clue 6: Mrs. Brisbane is on her feet and in a whirl.
Clue 7: She is performing very well. Mrs. Brisbane definitely must be at ballet school!

I had plenty of clues, but they didn't help me understand why Mrs. Brisbane would leave the class to learn ballet, especially with all the problems my friends were having.

And I didn't know how one small hamster—me— could solve their problems all by myself.

I *had* helped Kelsey. She hadn't bumped into anyone all week, and I'd heard her telling her friends about ballet class.

On the other paw, Hurry-Up-Harry seemed to have forgotten everything Mrs. Brisbane had taught him about getting back to class on time. Tell-the-Truth-Thomas was stretching the truth farther and farther every day and losing friends. And even though I knew why Forgetful-Phoebe was so forgetful, I couldn't think of what to do about it.

It was still a mystery to me why Mr. E. didn't do a little more teaching. After all, he was a teacher. He needed help, too.

It was quiet in the room now—so quiet, I could hear the big clock on the wall tick away the seconds.

TICK-TICK-TICK. TICK-TICK-TICK. I wished that clock would STOP-STOP-STOP because it reminded me of Phoebe's watch.

"Og, I sure wish I could find Phoebe's watch," I squeaked to my friend.

Suddenly, Og wasn't quiet anymore.

"BOING-BOING-BOING!" he twanged.

"You're right," I said. "I *should* find it."

"BOING!"

"I *must* find it."

"BOING-BOING!"

"I *will* find it!" I stomped my paw.

"BOING-BOING-TWANG!" Og splashed around in his water.

Now I just had to figure out *how* to do it.

HUMPHREY'S DETECTIONARY: One mystery, like what happened to your teacher, can lead to another mystery, like why the substitute teacher isn't really teaching.

The Case of the Wandering Watch

When Aldo looked around the room that night, he shook his head—again.

"What a wreck," he said. "Room Twenty-six was always the neatest classroom in the whole school. Now it's the messiest."

Once again, Mr. E. had not bothered to ask the students to clean up. In fact, when Helpful-Holly started to collect all the art supplies, he'd stopped her. "We have to use them tomorrow," he'd said. "Just leave them out."

Of course, they didn't have to leave paper scraps and glops of glue and piles of shiny glitter everywhere.

But Aldo went to work and soon the floor was clean, the art supplies were stacked and the student tables were straightened.

When Aldo sat down to eat dinner with us, he said, "Guys, I sure hope Mrs. Brisbane is back soon. I'll bet you do, too."

"Do you think she'll be back, Aldo?" I squeaked. "Or will she become a famous ballet dancer?"

"I know you think she's not coming back, Humphrey, but she is," Aldo assured me.

I was happy to hear that!

"But this messy room, that's nothing," Aldo said. "You should see all the stuff kids leave lying around. I take it all to the lost and found. Coats, socks, even shoes. Wouldn't you notice you were missing one shoe? Jewelry and toys. Lots of notebooks and pencils. Why, once I even found a tuba! That's a huge musical instrument." Aldo chuckled. "I can't imagine losing a tuba, but there it was. No name on it, either. I took it to the lost and found. I take everything to the lost and found."

"Really? That gives me a GREAT-GREAT-GREAT idea!" I squeaked.

Personally, I keep a close eye on my property: my wheel, sleeping hut, hamster ball, water bottle, food dish, climbing tree and ladder. I know where everything in my cage belongs, including my poo—which is only in my special poo corner—and the food I hide in my bedding. And of course, I always make sure my notebook and pencil are in their place.

Aldo pushed a lovely bit of cauliflower through the bars of my cage. "Time to move on," he said.

I watched out the window after he left, waiting for his car to leave the parking lot.

There was a big orange moon that looked a lot like a Halloween pumpkin. And the man in the moon looked like a jack-o'-lantern.

In the moonlight, I could see that the trees had lost most of their leaves. It was almost time for Halloween, all right.

Once Aldo was gone, I raced out of my cage.

"Og, Phoebe's watch must be in the lost and found," I squeaked. "I'd like to go get it, but Thomas said there were claws and hands and snakes in there."

"BOING-BOING!" Og replied.

"I know. Thomas does exaggerate sometimes. And Aldo didn't mention any of those things," I said.

"BOING-BOING-BOING-BOING!"

I don't really understand frog language, but I could tell what Og was trying to say.

"You're right," I admitted. "I think I have to go."

"BOING!"

"But first, I have to find Mrs. Wright's office, because that's where the lost and found is," I explained.

Og dived down into his water with an impressive splash.

I scurried down the leg of the table and headed toward the door. "Wish me luck!" I squeaked.

"BOING-BOING," Og said.

I slid through the narrow space under the door and there I was, out in the hallway of Longfellow School.

It's dark in the hallway at night, of course, but there are little lights along the way, so I could see where I was going.

I remembered that Mrs. Wright had said that the lost and found was in her office, inside the gym.

I've been to the library, the playground, the principal's office. But I've never, ever seen the gym.

I hurried past the other classrooms, took the turn

down another hallway, past Principal Morales's office, and past the cafeteria. That was as far as I'd ever gone in my nighttime adventures at Longfellow School. But that night, I saw that the hallway took another turn past the cafeteria.

I was in uncharted territory when I saw two gigantic doors. I stopped and looked up.

The sign on one door read *Gymnasium*.

Gym was in the word, so this must be it.

The doors were tall and looked heavy, but there was a narrow space below them. It was a little tight, but I squeezed through.

Even in the dim lighting, I could see that the gym was enormous! Of course, everything looks large to a small hamster, but this was the biggest room I'd ever seen. Ever!

It was TALL-TALL-TALL and WIDE-WIDE-WIDE. I'm not sure what they did in the gym, but there were hoops with nets on poles at either end and a shiny wooden floor. There was a big clock. And a huge sign with numbers on it.

As large as the gym was . . . and as little as I am, I was determined to find Phoebe's watch. There was a smaller door to the right of the main doors. I looked up and saw a sign that said *Mrs. Wright*.

The space under the door was unsqueakably narrow. I took a deep breath, exhaled and then pushed. Ooof! At first I didn't go through at all. But I gave another big push and suddenly, there I was in Mrs. Wright's office.

Now all I had to do was find the lost and found!

One wall had a cabinet with a big lock on it. I hoped that wasn't the lost and found, since I didn't know how to open a lock without a key. Luckily, the sign on it read *Equipment*.

I looked around and saw a desk against the opposite wall. On the shelf next to the desk there was another sign: *Lost and Found*.

"That's it!" I squeaked, even though there was no one around to hear me. At least I hoped there was no one around to hear me!

There was a stack of boxes next to Mrs. Wright's desk. I was able to climb them like steps and make my way to her desktop.

I paused to catch my breath, and I suddenly realized that Mrs. Wright wouldn't be happy to see me on her desk.

Mrs. Wright liked to see everything in its place. And she thought my place was in my cage.

Then I saw something terrible: MRS. WRIGHT'S WHISTLE! It was lying right there on top of her desk.

Funny, I'd always imagined that she wore that whistle everywhere. But I guess she went home without it. (Lucky for her family.)

It was silver and shiny and hard. I walked right up to it—so close I could see my reflection in it.

"You're not so scary!" I squeaked.

The whistle didn't say anything. I hadn't expected an answer, but still, I was relieved.

"You're not so big!" I yelled at the whistle.

Again, the whistle was silent.

"You're not so loud!" I yelled again.

The room stayed QUIET-QUIET-QUIET.

I could have stayed there a lot longer just yelling at that loud, rude whistle, but I had work to do.

Mrs. Wright's desk was tidy, and so was the lost-and-found shelf.

As neat as it was, I thought about the creepy things Thomas said he'd seen, so I decided to check it out from the desk first. I didn't see anything like a snake or a severed hand. Or even anything large, like the tuba Aldo mentioned.

What I did see were large plastic bins labeled *Clothing, Notebooks, Pens and Pencils, Books, Lunch Boxes, Jewelry, Other.*

Jewelry? Phoebe's watch could be in that bin.

I was able to hop directly from the desk to the lost-and-found shelf. As I hurried toward the jewelry bin, I could see through the little holes in the other boxes I passed.

In the clothing bin, I saw a sweater with blue polka dots, one striped sock, a green mitten, a pink backpack, a single red sneaker.

The next bin held dozens of pens, pencils, notebooks, a dictionary, and a book of music.

Then there was the bin filled with plastic lunch boxes and a thermos.

I finally reached the bin marked *Jewelry* and stopped to peer inside.

OH-OH-OH! There were chains of gold and silver, sparkly rings and those things girls wear in their hair and big, bright shiny things.

But I was only looking for one thing: Phoebe's watch. I needed to take a closer look.

I scrambled up the side of the bin, clinging to the edges of the holes. When I got to the top, I crossed my paws, held my breath . . . and dived right in!

I landed with a CLATTER-CLATTER-CLATTER and began to make my way through a sea of jewelry. It wasn't easy, because the items kept shifting beneath my toes.

I poked around with my paws and carefully began to dig through the tangle of rings, bracelets and necklaces. If only their owners had thought to check the lost and found!

Then I spied something round that had numbers on it in a circle. Yep, that was a watch all right. I liked the red band and the stars in between the numbers. I flipped it over. There was no name on it except Timewell, which I think was the name of the company that made the watch. At least I didn't know of any students at Longfellow School named Timewell.

It was a very nice watch, but it didn't fit Phoebe's description.

After some more poking, I found another round clock face. I tugged it out of the pile. It had a gold band, and in the center of the clock face was a smiling yellow flower. There was no name at all on the back of that watch.

I heard Phoebe's voice in my head. "My daisy watch," she'd called it.

Even Kelsey had called it "your daisy watch."

Well, a daisy is a yellow flower. This had to be Phoebe's watch!

To humans, I'm sure a child's watch doesn't seem too big, but it looked HUGE-HUGE-HUGE to me! I tried using my teeth to drag it an inch or two, but I soon realized that if I dragged it all the way back to the classroom, it would probably get scratched and dented.

I might get a little scratched and dented, too.

So I stopped and looked at the watch. The band was a stretchy circle, and it wasn't very big.

I put my front paws into the center of the circle and lifted one side over the back of my head. The band just fit around my middle. I took a few steps and was relieved that the watch didn't fall off.

Getting out of the bin took all my strength, because the watch made my body heavier.

Once I was out, I scurried across the shelf and leaped onto the desk. The weight of the watch made me slide and I just missed running into Mrs. Wright's whistle. Scary!

I came to a stop next to a pad of paper that had this word on it: *Military*.

Normally, I wouldn't have paid attention, but I'd just

heard Phoebe talking about her parents being away in the military and how much she missed them.

So I took a closer look. The paper read:

MKC: MILITARY KIDS CLUB

A brand-new club!
If you are a student with a parent in the military,
join us for weekly fun outings, tasty treats,
thoughtful discussion groups and a chance
to make friends with kids who are just like you!

There was a telephone number to call at the bottom. The Military Kids Club sounded perfect for Phoebe. She needed fun outings, and if she had friends to talk to who were going through the same things she was, maybe she would be able to relax. Maybe she wouldn't be so forgetful.

And everyone—even me—loves tasty treats!

But how could I get the information to Phoebe? I certainly couldn't carry a whole pad of paper back to Room 26.

Gently, I took the bottom edge of the top paper and tugged. It tore off the pad and I could see that there were identical notes beneath it.

So with the note for Phoebe in my teeth and her watch around my body, I started down the stair-step boxes but—whoa! The heavy watch made me feel all wobbly and I had to slow way down. I landed hard on the floor and made my way to the door.

I'd forgotten how small the space was under the door. With the watch around my middle, I couldn't fit. So I wiggled my way out of the watch and pushed it under the door.

I squeezed through the gap next. Once I was on the other side, I put the watch back on.

The trip back *from* the lost and found took twice as long as the trip *to* the lost and found, and the watch felt heavier and heavier with every step.

When I got back to Room 26, I had to push the watch under the door again.

By the time I finally slid under the door to Room 26, it was already getting light outside.

"I found it, Og!" I squeaked.

Of course, as soon as I opened my mouth, the paper fell out, but I managed to grab it with my teeth again.

"BOING-BOING-BOING-BOING!" Og replied. He must have been awfully worried about me while I was gone.

There was no time to waste, and I was exhausted. But I still had to make sure Phoebe got the watch.

"BOING-BOING!" Og warned.

I looked up at the clock. School would start soon, and I didn't want to be caught outside of my cage!

It would take a long time to climb all the way to Phoebe's table, leave the watch and get back down again.

I made a quick decision and headed to our table by the window.

There was the blinds cord. Swinging myself back up to the table is always tricky, but with Phoebe's watch (which now seemed to weigh a ton) and the paper in my mouth, I knew it would be harder than ever.

What I didn't expect was that the weight of the watch would make me swing faster than usual. It was a wild ride and my tummy felt queasy and uneasy.

Whew! I leaped onto the tabletop and slid FAST-FAST-FAST past Og's tank and right up to my door.

I wiggled my way out of the watch and left it on top of the MKC paper right in front of my cage.

"I got the watch, Og!" I said. "I'll tell you more later."

Then I darted inside, pulled the door behind me and ran into my sleeping hut.

In seconds, I was fast asleep.

HUMPHREY'S DETECTIONARY: Surprisingly, while you're solving one mystery, like where to find a watch, you might find a solution to another mystery, like how to help a friend.

11

The Case of the Creepy Classroom

As soon as the morning bell rang, I leaped out of my sleeping hut because I wanted to make sure Phoebe found the watch and the MKC notice.

While I was waiting for her to arrive, Thomas came in and tapped Just-Joey on the shoulder. He had a big friendly smile and said, "Hey, Joey . . . want to shoot some hoops after school?"

Joey looked surprised. He didn't smile at all. "I'm busy," he said.

"Maybe tomorrow?" Thomas asked.

Joey shook his head. "I don't think so." And then he walked away.

Thomas wasn't smiling anymore.

I think Thomas is a nice boy. I know for a fact that Joey is a nice boy. But I didn't think Joey was being very nice to Thomas.

"What's going on, Og?" I asked my froggy friend.

"BOING-BOING!" he replied.

"I'm not sure I want any more mysteries to solve," I squeaked.

Og dived into the water and splashed around.

Just then, Phoebe came into the classroom and went straight to her table.

"Over here, Phoebe!" I squeaked at the top of my lungs.

She didn't pay any attention, so I jumped up and down.

"PHOEBE!" I screamed. "OVER HERE!"

She still didn't respond, so I climbed up to the top of my cage.

"WILL SOMEBODY PLEASE TELL PHOEBE TO COME OVER HERE?" I shrieked.

I heard Rosie giggle. "Look at Humphrey. He's acting silly!"

She rolled her wheelchair over to the table for a closer look. Simon, Joey and Kelsey rushed over.

"Phoebe, come see Humphrey," Kelsey said.

Thank goodness!

Finally, Phoebe came over, too.

Since an audience had gathered around me, I decided to give them a show.

Clinging to the top bars of my cage, I made my way, paw over paw, across to the other side.

"Go, Humphrey, go!" Simon cheered me on.

"Where's he going, anyway?" Rosie asked.

I knew exactly where I was going—to the side of my cage near Phoebe's watch and the MKC paper. I took a deep breath and I dropped down into the soft bedding.

I did a double flip-flop. I hadn't planned on it, but my friends all said, "Oooh!"

I looked over at the watch and the paper, crossed my paws and hoped.

"Hey, Phoebe, isn't this your watch?" Kelsey asked.

Phoebe stared at the watch. "It is!" She picked it up. "But I looked here yesterday. How did I miss it?"

"Maybe the custodian found it," Rosie suggested.

Phoebe put on her watch and smiled.

I crossed my paws tighter.

Kelsey picked up the MKC notice. "It was sitting on this," she said.

She handed the paper to Phoebe, who stared at it and stared some more.

The bell rang and the students all headed for their chairs.

Phoebe slipped the paper into her pocket.

It worked! I could finally uncross my paws. Phoebe had her watch back, and maybe she'd call that number for MKC.

I was proud of myself, but my joy didn't last long, because when I looked over at Thomas, he was staring at his desk and looking about as unhappy as a human could look.

"Class, get ready for a ton of fun!" Mr. E. announced.

I wasn't in the mood for fun, so I crawled into my sleeping hut and had a nice dream about Phoebe's daisy watch.

When I awoke, I thought I was having a bad dream. In fact, I thought I was having a nightmare!

There were ghosts hanging from the ceiling! There were witches and broomsticks and black cats flying above the bulletin board! And there were leering pumpkins of every shape and size pinned on the board.

"Eeek!" I squeaked.

I don't think anybody heard me.

"I'll bet this is the best-decorated room in all of Longfellow School," Mr. E. told my friends.

To squeak the truth, he was probably right. But I didn't think looking at those hideous grinning pumpkin faces and ghastly ghosts all night long would be best for me.

"And don't forget, there'll be a costume party on Halloween next week," Mr. E. reminded the class.

"Eeek!" I squeaked again.

As if my paws weren't already full (of problems), now I had to come up with a costume.

Humans just don't realize how much a classroom hamster has to do.

❧⚘❧

After school, Mr. Morales came into the classroom. "Nice decorations, Ed," he said.

Mr. E. looked very proud. Mr. Morales took a piece of paper out of his pocket. "Have you got a moment?"

"Sure," Mr. E. said.

The two men sat in some student chairs. Grown-up humans always look funny sitting in those small chairs.

"How have things been going with the class?" the principal asked.

"Great," Mr. E. said. "The kids are the best."

Mr. Morales nodded. "Yes, and I can tell they like you a lot."

Mr. E. smiled and I think his red hair glowed a little brighter.

"But there have been a few problems," Mr. Morales continued.

"Yes, there have!" I squeaked. "Problems like Phoebe-Harry-Kelsey-Simon-Rosie-Holly-Thomas!"

I know all that the principal heard was "SQUEAK-SQUEAK-SQUEAK," and it made him laugh.

"Yes, Humphrey, I know you're listening," he said.

Mr. E. cleared his throat. "What, um, problems?"

The principal looked down at the paper. "Well, Mrs. Wright has complained about some safety issues, some injuries, a problem with noise. And a problem with students roaming the halls during class."

"Oh," Mr. E. said. "I guess Mrs. Wright and I don't see eye to eye."

Mr. Morales smiled. "Mrs. Wright does like to follow the rules. But rules are there for a reason, after all."

Mr. E. nodded nervously. "Yes, I understand."

If he understood, why didn't he follow them? That was part of the mystery of Mr. E.

"And a few parents have called to say that they're concerned about a lack of homework," Mr. Morales continued.

Mr. E. chuckled. "I'll bet the students haven't complained about that."

"No," Principal Morales replied. "But we're here to teach the children. I believe that learning is fun, but there's work involved, too."

Mr. E. nodded. And nodded some more. He looked so nervous, even his red hair looked pale.

"And then there's Mrs. Brisbane." Mr. Morales wasn't smiling anymore. "She's wondering if you're keeping up with her lesson plans. She said you haven't called her with questions."

"Oh," Mr. E. said. "Well, I've been following the lesson plans but adding my own touches. Maybe I haven't been following them closely enough."

At least Mr. E. was honest. I liked that about him.

"The district-wide math test is coming up. Are the students prepared for that?" Mr. Morales asked.

"Not completely," Mr. E. said. "Not yet."

"Ed, I want to give you a chance. You're a new teacher, and I know you really want to continue," Mr. Morales said. "But the learning comes first."

"It certainly does!" I squeaked.

"BOING-BOING-BOING-BOING!" Og agreed.

"Are you letting me go?" Mr. E. asked.

"No, Ed," Mr. Morales said. "I think you can be a good teacher. But I need to see a change starting tomorrow."

"Yes, yes, I'll change," Mr. E. said. "Thank you for giving me another chance. I won't let you down."

The two men shook hands and Mr. Morales left.

Once he was alone again, Mr. E. began to mutter something I couldn't understand. I did hear the word "failed."

I know that my fellow classmates don't want to fail. Maybe teachers don't want to fail, either.

After a while, he got up and paced around the room.

"Don't give up," I squeaked. I was trying to helpful.

I guess Mr. E. heard my squeaks, because he looked my way.

"I'll tell you one thing, I'm not giving up yet," he said.

He sounded very determined, which gave me hope.

"Take out the lesson plans," I squeaked. "In the binder. In the drawer!"

I didn't think he was likely to listen to me, since he thought of me as an "it." But surprisingly, he marched over to the desk, opened the drawer and took out the binder.

He stuffed the binder into his large sack. Then he came over to the table where Og and I live.

"You have it easy," he said. "You're just classroom pets. Everybody loves you and you don't have to worry about tests."

Then he stared out the window, his shoulders slumped. He sighed once or twice.

After a while I couldn't stand it. "You can do a better job!" I squeaked. "TRY-TRY-TRY!"

Mr. E. looked down at me and *almost* smiled.

"Would you like to switch jobs with me, Humphrey?" he asked.

I think it was the first time he used my name.

"I could sit in your cage and take naps and you'd teach the class," he said.

I was sorry to hear that he thought all that I did was sit in my cage and take naps. But then, he didn't know about the lock-that-doesn't-lock.

"I really like my job," I squeaked. I was too polite to say that I didn't think Mr. E. would be a very good classroom pet.

"I really like my job," Mr. E. said. "And I want to make this work."

"I want this to work, too!" I replied.

Just then Ms. Mac walked in. Why do good things always happen when Ms. Mac walks in?

"Hi, Ed," she said. "How's it going?"

Mr. E. sighed. "Not very well, I'm afraid."

"What happened?" Ms. Mac asked.

"Mr. Morales just told me there have been a lot of complaints about my teaching. Too much noise, not enough homework . . . and Mrs. Brisbane doesn't think I'm following her lesson plans," he explained.

"Are you?" Ms. Mac asked in the friendliest way possible.

Mr. E. shook his head. "Yes, and, uh, no."

Ms. Mac said, "Oh." She came a little closer to my

cage and leaned down. "Hi, Humphrey," she said with a wink.

"I really want to be a teacher," Mr. E. said. "There were no job openings, so I signed up to be a substitute."

"That's how I got started," Ms. Mac said.

Yes, and if she hadn't, I wouldn't have my wonderful job!

"I've never told anybody what happened," Mr. E. said.

Ms. Mac smiled. "I'm a good listener."

Mr. E. nodded. "Okay."

"Listen up, Og," I squeaked to my neighbor. "Maybe we'll solve the mystery of Mr. E."

"BOING-BOING!" Og agreed.

"My first day as a substitute was a nightmare," he said. "I tried to teach the kids, but they wouldn't be quiet, wouldn't sit down, wouldn't listen to a word I said. When I tried to give them homework, they threw paper wads at me."

"What?" I squeaked. "That was RUDE-RUDE-RUDE!"

"BOING-BOING-BOING!" Og was as shocked as I was.

Ms. Mac was surprised, too. "Was that at Longfellow School?" she asked.

"No," Mr. E. said. "I tell you, I was ready to give up teaching forever. And I decided that the next time I got an assignment, I'd make everything fun. If the kids liked me, maybe they'd behave better."

"I understand," Ms. Mac said. "But you can have fun and learning at the same time. Students can have respect for you and like you at the same time. Look at Mrs. Brisbane!"

"Yes, look!" I squeaked.

"I wish I knew her," Mr. E. said. "This is such a great class, and I don't think I've lived up to her standards. But it was so awful to know that the students in that first class didn't like me."

You'd think I'd have learned it by now, but sometimes I forget: teachers are humans!

"I have an idea," Ms. Mac said. "I'm going to visit a friend tonight, and I'd like you to come along. Are you free?"

"Yes," Mr. E. said. "But I have to prepare for tomorrow."

Ms. Mac smiled mysteriously. "I think you can do both."

Before long, they were gone.

"Og, I'm sorry to say I thought Mr. E. just didn't care," I told my friend when we were alone. "I'm glad I was wrong. But I wonder if Mrs. Brisbane still cares."

"BOING?" Og sounded confused.

"She's abandoned her students to go off and become a ballerina," I explained. "That doesn't seem right!"

There. I'd said it. I love Mrs. Brisbane with all the heart a small hamster has to offer. But I had to admit, I was *piewhacked* by her behavior. And a little disappointed, too.

114

I guess Og was disappointed, too, because he dived into the water and splashed wildly.

I'm not one for splashing, so I hopped on my wheel for a good, long spin.

HUMPHREY'S DETECTIONARY: When you solve a mystery, you might learn some shocking information (involving badly behaved students).

The Case of the New Mr. E.

As the light in the room grew darker that evening, the pumpkins on the wall grew brighter. For some reason, those jack-o'-lanterns really bothered me.

Aldo liked them, though. When he came in to clean that night, he said, "Whoa! I almost thought I was in the wrong room." He stopped and admired all the decorations. "They did a real good job. Speaking of Halloween, I have a present for you, Humphrey."

I LOVE-LOVE-LOVE presents!

He wheeled his cart to the middle of the room. Then he reached into his lunch sack and pulled something out. "Maria helped me with this," Aldo explained as he walked toward my cage.

He opened the door and put something orange in my cage. "A little Halloween treat," he said.

In front of me was a tiny little jack-o'-lantern. It was actually a piece of pumpkin, with carrots and seeds that made a little face.

It looked perfectly hamster-licious!

"Thank you, thank you—a million times," I squeaked excitedly.

"It's my pleasure," Aldo replied.

I started to nibble on the pumpkin right away while Aldo gave Og his nightly Froggy Food Sticks.

Poor Og. I guess he'll never know how tasty pumpkin is, especially the seeds.

When Aldo was ready to leave, he said, "I've got a joke for you two. What do ghosts eat on their cereal?"

"I have no idea," I said.

Og didn't say a thing. Not even BOING.

"Booberries!" Then Aldo burst out laughing and kept on chuckling as he rolled his cart out the door.

After he'd gone, when I looked up at the row of pumpkins on the wall, they didn't look scary.

They just looked yummy!

~⁓~

"Class, it's time to begin," Mr. E. announced the next morning. "We have a lot to do today."

"Can we play Mathketball?" Simon asked.

"Not right now," Mr. E. answered.

"Word War?" Rosie asked.

"Not today," Mr. E. said. "We've got a lot of work to do."

There were a few groans, but not many.

"We're going to start with Mrs. Brisbane's mystery words," he said. "Take out a sheet of paper."

Mr. E. still had small round glasses and red hair. But

this was a different Mr. E. than I'd seen before. This was a real teacher.

Besides, I was HAPPY-HAPPY-HAPPY that we were going back to mystery words.

I knew what *piewhack* meant. And *pizzazz*.

But today, Mr. E. gave us a new word to figure out: *pursizzle*.

I wondered if it meant a hot handbag.

He wrote this sentence on the board:

When you go to the store, please get some pursizzle for tomorrow's lunches.

Gosh, *pursizzle* had to be some kind of food. But it could be anything: carrots, apples, celery or other crunchy things.

Then he wrote another sentence:

My grandmother spent the afternoon teaching me how to bake pursizzle.

I don't think a grandmother would spend a whole afternoon teaching somebody how to bake a carrot or an apple. (I like them raw.)

The third sentence was:

My favorite breakfast is pursizzle with jam.

Jam. It's a sweet, fruity spread. I know that. And as far as I knew, humans usually ate jam on—bread!

Pursizzle was *bread*!

I got 100 percent on my assignment. My friends were all shouting out "bread," so they got 100 percent, too.

I was most excited because Mr. E. was following Mrs. Brisbane's lesson plan, and as far as I could tell, everybody still liked him.

Personally, I liked him a little more than I had the day before.

I didn't have much time to think about *pursizzle* with jam because Mr. E. then went into a math lesson that didn't involved basketballs or running or shouting. My friends worked hard and didn't talk unless they were called on.

Just before recess, Mr. E. talked about Egypt. He had me on the edge of my seat—er, cage—talking about pyramids, mummies and the Nile River. I tell you, I was shivering and quivering during that lesson.

And when my friends went out to play, Mr. E. sat at Mrs. Brisbane's desk and studied lesson plans in her binder.

We got so much done that day, I'm not sure Mrs. Brisbane could have kept up . . . but my classmates and I did.

Mr. E. even gave out homework assignments. *Real* homework. No one complained because he explained why it was important.

Late in the afternoon, Helpful-Holly reminded Mr. E. that he needed to choose who would take me home for the weekend.

Mr. E. asked my friends to raise their hands if they hadn't taken me home yet and thought their parents would give permission.

A lot of hands went up. How was Mr. E. going to choose?

He looked at the clock. "I think we have time for a quick spelling bee to decide."

He asked Rosie, Joey, Tall-Paul, Thomas and Sophie to spell different words.

They all got through the first round. On the second round, Rosie missed on the word *symbol*. (I was surprised there was a *y* in it, too.)

On the third round, Tall-Paul missed on the word *misery*. I completely understood, because the *s* does sound like a *z*.

Sophie went down on the word *mystify*. I would have, too!

It was down to Joey and Thomas. And for the next two rounds, neither of them missed a word. They were difficult words, too: *disease, fierce, schedule*!

The spelling bee was suddenly very exciting, and it was almost time for the bell to ring.

"I'll tell you what," Mr. E. said. "You've done such a great job, would you agree to share Humphrey?"

The boys both looked puzzled. I was a little concerned, too. I hoped they weren't planning to split me in half!

"Thomas could have him Friday night. Then Joey could pick him up at Thomas's house on Saturday and have Humphrey Saturday night," Mr. E. explained. "Would your families agree to that?"

Neither boy looked happy. But they both nodded.

"Bring back notes from your parents tomorrow," Mr. E. told them just as the bell rang.

"How did it go?" Ms. Mac asked after school.

"Not bad." Mr. E. smiled. "We got a lot done and nobody threw anything at me. Thanks for taking me along last night. I think I'm on the right track now."

"Great," Ms. Mac said. "And the Halloween surprise is really going to be something. We just need to make sure no one finds out our secret."

"Finds out what?" I squeaked.

"BOING-BOING!" Og twanged.

Ms. Mac must have heard us, because she laughed.

"No one must find out . . . even Humphrey and Og!" she said.

When Mr. E. and Ms. Mac left for the day, I was annoyed.

"It's not nice to keep secrets," I told Og. "And it's especially not nice to keep secrets from classroom pets!"

"BOING-BOING-BOING-BOING," Og agreed.

But I had something else on my mind besides the

Halloween surprise. I could tell that Joey didn't want to be around Thomas. I wasn't sure why, but I think it had to do with the way Thomas exaggerated.

They should have been friends, but they weren't. And I was *piewhacked* about how to help them.

I had another problem to think about: my costume. I'd felt so proud to win the prize for Best Costume last Halloween. And I hoped I'd win it again.

⌒⌒

Friday was a busy day . . . and a day that made me HAPPY-HAPPY-HAPPY.

We learned more about Egypt and a new kind of math problem and we got a new vocabulary list. The day went by in a hurry because we were so busy.

At the very end of the day, Mr. E. made a special announcement. If the class all did well on our math test on Monday, he'd finish reading "The Red-Headed-League."

Everybody cheered at that news! No one cheered louder than me.

⌒⌒

I was really looking forward to meeting Thomas's dad. After all, according to his son, Mr. True was a juggler-airplane-pilot-ship's-captain-detective!

When he came to pick us up from school, he just looked like a regular nice dad.

"Do you mind sharing Humphrey this weekend?" he asked as he drove us home from school.

"Not really," Thomas said. "Maybe when Joey comes over tomorrow, we can shoot some hoops."

122

"Sure," Mr. True said. "I'll take you to the park."

I wasn't sure if Joey would like that, but I crossed my paws and hoped that he'd say yes.

When we got to the house, I was suddenly a little nervous. So far this school year, Thomas had told a lot of stories about his shark teeth collection, the gigantic fish he'd caught and huge spiders and colossal snakes. *And* all those tall tales about his dad.

Luckily, I didn't see any spiders, snakes, or fish—with or without teeth—at his house.

Thomas's dad helped get me set up. His little sister, Theresa, came in to watch me. I spun on my wheel for her, which made her laugh.

Then Thomas's mom brought me a celery treat.

Later that night, they all watched me roll around in my hamster ball. While I rolled, I wished I could help the boys become friends. All that rolling helped me think, and before long, I had a Plan that would force them to spend time together, at least for a little while.

I crossed my paws and hoped it would work.

If they got to know each other better, maybe Joey would find out what I knew: Thomas was a nice, normal boy. And Thomas would find out that if he wanted friends, he needed to stop exaggerating and tell the truth. Otherwise, how could anyone trust what he said?

HUMPHREY'S DETECTIONARY: If you don't have a violin like Sherlock Holmes, rolling in a hamster ball can also help you think.

The Case of the Battling Boys

On Saturday afternoon, I was rolling around the living room in my hamster ball when the doorbell rang.

Thomas ran to open the door and said, "Hi, Joey."

It was time for my Plan. I started running like crazy in my ball so it rolled and rolled and rolled way, way under the couch, where it was dark and a little dusty. Perfect!

Thomas and Joey were talking, but their voices were hard to hear because there was a piece of cloth around the bottom of the couch that reached to the floor.

"Hey, Joey. My dad said he'd drive us to the park. We could shoot some hoops there," Thomas said.

"No," Joey said. "My mom's waiting in the car."

"My dad would take you back later," Thomas said. "He could talk to your mom."

I thought I heard Joey say "no" again. Then he asked, "Where's Humphrey?"

Thomas said something I couldn't understand and then Joey said, "Well, he must be around here somewhere."

They said something about searching for me. Then all I heard were footsteps clomping all over the room.

"I used to have a hamster named Giggles," Joey said. "He loved his hamster ball. Humphrey reminds me of him."

Then Thomas said, "*I* used to have a pet ostrich! He giggled, too."

"No way," Joey said.

"I did!" Thomas insisted. "His name was Ozzie."

Joey sighed. "Let's just find Humphrey."

The boys were quiet again except for their footsteps.

"He must be under something," Joey said.

More footsteps. Then Thomas said, "Not under the chair."

Even more footsteps. Then Joey said, "What about the couch?"

Before I knew it, a hand lifted up the cloth. Thomas and Joey were staring right at me.

"Humphrey!" Thomas said. "What are you doing there?"

I didn't dare squeak the truth, so I stayed silent.

Joey reached way, way back and grabbed the hamster ball. "Where's his cage?"

"In my room," Thomas said.

Joey carried me to Thomas's room and put me back in my cage. "Okay, Humphrey. We're ready to go," he told me.

"Wait," Thomas said. "Don't you want to come

shoot some hoops with my dad and me? He used to be in the NBA."

"NBA? Look, I just don't want to, okay?" Joey said.

I was surprised to hear Joey talk like that. Just-Joey usually got along with everyone.

"What's wrong with you?" Thomas asked.

"Why are you always telling lies?" Joey asked. "Your dad wasn't in the NBA and he's not a detective or an airline pilot or any of that stuff, right?"

Thomas hesitated. "No," he admitted. "But he's in the transportation business. He sells cars!"

"You don't have to make up all that stuff. You're lucky to have a dad around. Not everybody does," Joey said. "My dad lives far away and I don't get to see him much. But I don't lie about him."

"Sorry," Thomas said. He sounded sorry.

I was sorry that Joey didn't get to see his dad much, too.

But Joey wasn't finished with Thomas. "What about the lost and found?"

Thomas rolled his eyes. "It was kind of creepy in there. But maybe the severed hand was just a glove."

"And the ostrich?" Joey asked.

Thomas laughed. "I did have an ostrich named Ozzie! But it was a toy I had when I was little."

Joey grinned. "I believe that. And the shark teeth?"

"That's true," Thomas said. "I'll show you."

He opened a drawer and handed a box to Joey. "Here they are."

Joey's eyes got really big when he looked inside the box. "Wow. These really *are* shark teeth."

"My uncle gave them to me," Thomas said. "He's in the navy. And that's true."

I scrambled to get a peek at the shark teeth. Eeek! They looked unsqueakably sharp!

Joey stared at the teeth. "Do you know what kind they are?"

Thomas shook his head.

"The library has a book on sharks. We could look them up," Joey said.

"Together?" Thomas asked.

Just-Joey grinned. "Yeah, if you don't make stuff up."

Thomas nodded and said, "I just like to make things sound more interesting."

"You don't need to," Joey answered.

Thomas seemed surprised. "I don't?"

"Just be you. Just-Thomas," Joey said.

Thomas thought for a second. "Okay. So, do you want to shoot hoops before we go to the library?" he asked.

Joey did, which made me feel GREAT-GREAT-GREAT. He went out and talked to his mom. Then Mr. True took Joey and Thomas away for a long time.

When they came back, they had a new idea. Joey would spend the night at Thomas's and they would look after me together.

That meant I wasn't going to Joey's house after all. I wasn't all that disappointed, since he had a dog named

Skipper who caught Frisbees in his teeth. I'd seen the tooth marks, so I'm pretty sure he wasn't exaggerating.

I'd rather be around shark's teeth with no shark attached than a dog with teeth still in its mouth.

And on Sunday, I was thrilled when Thomas and Joey studied for the big math test—together!

Before class started on Monday, Joey told his friends about Thomas's amazing shark tooth collection.

"You mean that was true?" Simon asked.

"Yes," Joey said. "It really was."

Then Thomas said, "I guess I exaggerated about some other things. Sorry about that. I just like a good story."

"Me too," Do-It-Now-Daniel said. "Especially Sherlock Holmes."

"Sherlock Holmes? We've got to do well on our test so we can hear the end of that story," Tall-Paul said.

"I studied," Harry said.

"Me too," Simon said.

"Yep, I did, too," Small-Paul said.

That was good news!

After attendance, Mr. E. got right to work and the math test began.

I watched my friends thinking, writing, erasing, writing some more.

After the test was over, my friends begged Mr. E. to grade them right away. So while they were at recess, he sat at Mrs. Brisbane's desk and marked each one. When he was finished, he smiled.

"Good," he said. "Very good."

"Did you hear that, Og?" I squeaked. I looked over just as my friend did a magnificent dive into his water. I guess he had heard.

When my classmates came back after recess, all eyes were on Mr. E.

"Well, class, I'm sorry to tell you . . ." Mr. E. paused. My friends looked VERY-VERY-VERY nervous.

". . . that I'm going to have to read you the rest of 'The Red-Headed League'!"

Everybody cheered, including me.

"You all did very well on the test," he said.

Naturally, with all that cheering, the door opened and there was Mrs. Wright.

"I could hear your class all the way down the hall," she said.

Still smiling, Mr. E. walked toward her. "I'm sorry, Mrs. Wright. We were celebrating the great job my students did on their math test."

Mrs. Wright looked surprised. "Oh. Well, that's good news."

"We'll cheer a little more quietly next time," Mr. E. said.

"Thank you, Mr. Edonopolous," Mrs. Wright replied. She actually smiled.

Humans can be very *piewhacking*.

After she left, Mr. E. said, "Mrs. Brisbane would be pleased with you."

Mrs. Brisbane would be pleased with us. That was nice to hear.

But I wasn't very pleased with Mrs. Brisbane. How could she start reading an exciting story and then run off and go to ballet school without even finishing it? Really, it was a mystery to me.

And then I remembered what she'd said in her letters: *To think, it was all because of Humphrey.*

What had I done? What had I said?

Maybe Sherlock Holmes, the great detective, would help me understand.

Mr. E. pulled a tall stool from the corner and moved it to the front of the classroom. He took off his sweater and everyone laughed. He had on a black T-shirt that had *Mr. E.* is red wavy letters and a cartoon of a man with bright red hair that looked a lot like him.

He sat on the stool and in a mysterious voice said, "A mystery read by Mr. E.!"

He opened the big red book and said, "And now, the exciting conclusion of 'The Adventure of the Red-Headed League.'" He began to read. He was an excellent story reader . . . every bit as good as Mrs. Brisbane!

It turns out that Mr. Jabez Wilson went to his strange job each evening and was paid well. Then one day when he came to work, the office was locked and a sign read *The Red-Headed League Is Dissolved.*

That's when he visited Sherlock Holmes (which was an unsqueakably good idea).

I don't want to give away the whole story, but Sherlock Holmes solved the puzzle and caught the bad guys in the act! And—what a surprise—the Red-Headed League turned out to be a trick!

Sherlock Holmes showed me that a detective can't always assume things are what they seem to be. Could I have been wrong about what happened to Mrs. Brisbane? I hoped that, one day, I'd find out.

"What did you think?" Mr. E. asked. "Did any of you figure it out?"

Thomas T. True's hand shot up in the air. "I did!"

"Really?" Mr. E. asked. "When?"

I saw Just-Joey turn to watch Thomas. I think he was pretty sure Thomas was going to exaggerate. Maybe Thomas noticed Joey's look, too.

Thomas grinned. "When you read us the ending!"

Everybody laughed, and Joey high-fived Thomas.

After he was finished with the story, Mr. E. gave us a lesson on Egypt, a lesson on writing sentences, and a new math problem. He even showed us different kinds of clouds with cool pictures on a projector.

We were BUSY-BUSY-BUSY.

Near the end of the day, Mr. Morales stopped by Room 26. He was wearing a tie with little gold stars all over it.

"I don't want to interrupt your studies," he said. "I

just want to say that I heard this class did a tremendous job on the math test today."

Mr. E. nodded. "They really did. Are you proud of yourselves?"

My classmates cheered and clapped. I hopped up and down and squeaked, "YES-YES-YES!"

"Congratulations, Mr. E. and class. Keep up the good work," the principal said.

I was unsqueakably proud of Mr. E.

It looked as if he was turning into a good teacher. And my friends still liked him.

I guess I liked him, too.

HUMPHREY'S DETECTIONARY: Sometimes a detective learns something surprising about himself. (He might even learn that someone he didn't like is really a good human after all.)

The Case of the Weird, Weird Witch

Mr. E. worked so hard the next few days that my class caught up with Mrs. Brisbane's lesson plans. But it wasn't all hard work. He also read us a fur-raising story about a secret code. And it turned out that the secret code was also a math problem!

During the day, I was busy trying to keep up with the lessons. At night, I'd make notes in my notebook so I'd remember what we'd learned in class.

But there was more than just schoolwork going on. Mr. E. talked to Hurry-Up-Harry about getting back to class on time, and suddenly, Harry wasn't late anymore.

One day, Phoebe came up to my cage smiling. She held up her wrist with the daisy watch on it.

"See, Humphrey, I still have it," she said. "And guess what? Yesterday after school, I went to a meeting of this new club. It's only for kids whose parents are in the military. We talked about our parents and we played a game and we're having a Halloween party, too!"

"That's pawsitively great!" I squeaked. I could tell Phoebe was feeling better already. And she remembered her homework all week, too.

Joey and Thomas were together all the time. I even heard them whispering about their Halloween costumes. They said something about "hats," or maybe it was "bats." And they also mentioned "grasses." Maybe they meant "glasses." Were they going to dress up as bats with glasses? Or wear hats made of grasses? You can never guess *what* humans will wear for Halloween.

There was so much talk about Halloween, I couldn't help thinking about last year's party. I didn't know much about Halloween then. All I knew was that humans wore costumes and that the class would have a party.

But last year we had a different class. We had a different teacher. And I was a different hamster.

Oh, I was still Humphrey. But I was just starting to learn about school.

Now, I knew a LOT-LOT-LOT more.

I just didn't know what my costume would be.

The night before Halloween, Aldo came into Room 26 and stopped. He looked around and said, "Will you look at that? It's almost as clean as when Mrs. Brisbane was here."

"And where is she now?" I squeaked loudly.

I guess Aldo didn't understand me.

"How do you like my costume?" Aldo twirled around.

He looked the same as usual. He had on a blue shirt and black pants and he was pushing his cleaning trolley.

"This *is* my costume! Get it?" Aldo roared with laughter, and I realized that he was joking.

I like jokes. I think most hamsters do.

"I need a costume, too," I squeaked.

"BOING-BOING!" Og agreed.

"I know you're excited," Aldo said. "I talked to Richie today. He's excited, too."

Richie was his nephew, and he'd been in Room 26 last year.

"He's going to be a monster," Aldo explained.

It was hard to imagine Richie as a monster. He was a very nice human. Maybe there are nice monsters, too. I'll bet there are.

When Aldo sat down to have his dinner, I was hoping for a pumpkin treat, and I wasn't disappointed.

"Trick or treat, buddy," he said.

"Thanks, Aldo. Trick or squeak!" I called after him.

～◦～

Later, when Aldo was gone, I told Og, "Tomorrow is Halloween."

"BOING-BOING!" he replied.

"I need a costume," I said, walking toward the edge of our table. "Don't you?"

"BOING-BOING-BOING-BOING!" He didn't seem to like the idea of wearing a costume.

"You don't have to wear a costume, Og. But I want one," I said. "I had an idea today when I was thinking about the Sherlock Holmes story. And I have a Plan."

Og dived into his water with a giant splash. I dashed away to keep from getting wet.

I slid down the table leg and scurried across the room to the shelves where the art supplies were stored.

Luckily, they were low to the ground, so I could easily scramble up the side of a bin and slip over the edge. Once I was inside, I found what I wanted. I gnawed and gnawed until I had exactly what I needed for my costume.

Holding my treasure in my mouth, I climbed up a stack of glue sticks, hopped on a tall jar of glitter and slid back over the edge.

I swung back up to the table and went straight to my cage. I hid my costume in my bedding and closed the cage door behind me.

"BOING-BOING!" Og twanged.

"My costume is a surprise, Og. You'll find out what it is tomorrow," I squeaked back at him. "*Everybody* will find out tomorrow."

There were no costumes on Halloween morning. There were just the usual lessons. But after lunch, Mr. E. sent everyone out of the room to change into their costumes. Simon's mom and Small-Paul's dad were there to help.

When the room was empty, Mr. E. turned toward Og and me and said, "You're about to have a *big* surprise."

"So are you!" I squeaked.

Then he left the room, too.

While the room was empty, I made sure my costume was still under my bedding.

It seemed like a LONG-LONG-LONG time before the door finally opened again.

In walked a tall pirate and a short ninja. I guessed they were Tall-Paul and Small-Paul.

Then a princess with a sparkling crown on her head came in. That was Holly.

More kids came into the classroom in amazing costumes. Phoebe wore a camouflage military uniform. Kelsey was a ballerina in a pink tutu. Her eye was back to normal, and she looked very graceful.

Then a very surprising pair came in. They were dressed alike in long coats and those deerstalker hats like Sherlock Holmes wore, and they carried huge magnifying glasses.

Thomas and Joey were both dressed like Sherlock Holmes. So they had been talking about hats and glasses, not bats and grasses!

Right behind them was Simon in a superhero costume with a blue cape, along with Harry, who was all wrapped in white like a mummy.

Then something amazing happened. A table rolled through the door. There was a plate on the table with a knife and fork next to it. And on the plate was Rosie's head!

"Eeek!" I squeaked.

Rosie smiled and everybody laughed. Someone had

put a box over her shoulders with a hole for her head. She had painted a tablecloth, and the plate, knife and fork were glued on.

It was the best costume I'd seen so far!

My friends sat at their tables and waited. Or in their tables, in Rosie's case.

We all waited quite a while before the door opened again.

I figured I'd see Mr. E., but that's not what I saw at all.

In came a grinning pumpkin head on a skinny skeleton body and a truly horrible old witch. She was all hunched over and leaned on a crooked wooden cane. Her face was hideous, with huge warts and a pointed nose and green skin.

The room was silent as they walked to the front of the room and faced us.

"How do witches tell time?" the pumpkin skeleton asked in a strange, high-pitched voice.

"With a witch-watch!" the witch answered. And then she cackled wildly. The sound made my fur stand on end.

"What do you call a nervous witch?" the pumpkin skeleton asked.

"A twitch!" the weird witch answered, and cackled loudly again.

I was about to go hide in my sleeping hut when the pumpkin skeleton asked another question.

"And which witch are you?" the pumpkin skeleton asked.

This time, the witch didn't answer.

"Class, who knows which witch this is?" the skeleton asked us.

For a few seconds, no one spoke. Or squeaked.

And then Small-Paul shouted, "Mrs. Brisbane!"

Mrs. Brisbane was a *witch*? And all this time, I thought she was a ballerina!

The witch reached up and took off her witchy face, which was just a mask.

And there was Mrs. Brisbane, smiling happily at us.

Everyone in the class cheered and clapped.

Og splashed loudly. "BOING-BOING-BOING-BOING!"

I climbed up to the top of my cage and shouted, "Welcome back!"

Mr. E. took off his pumpkin head and grinned.

"I'm so happy to see all of you," Mrs. Brisbane said in her regular voice. "Mr. E. came to visit me, and we planned this surprise for you. I'm so proud of how well you did on your math test."

The door opened and a mad scientist with wild white hair and a white coat came in, along with a clown with a round red nose and a pink-, blue- and green-striped wig.

"Happy Halloween!" The clown sounded just like Mrs. Wright. In fact, I was sure it was Mrs. Wright when I saw that the clown had a whistle around her neck.

"Welcome back!" The mad scientist sounded just like Mr. Morales.

"It's good to be back," Mrs. Brisbane said.

Still leaning on her stick, Mrs. Brisbane hobbled over to see Og and me.

"Of course, I missed my friends Humphrey and Og," she said.

"I'm so glad to see you!" I squeaked.

Og jumped for joy. "BOING!"

"Hi, Og. Hello, Humphrey," Mrs. Brisbane said. "You know, Humphrey, you're the cause of this."

My heart sank to my toes. "What did I do!?" I squeaked.

Our teacher turned to the class. "You see, I was running a little late for school that morning. I was already in my car when I realized I'd forgotten Humphrey's fresh vegetable treat. As I ran back to the house, my heel caught on the front step and I tumbled down and broke my ankle."

She lifted a corner of her long witch's skirt and showed us her cast.

"I'm unsqueakably sorry!" I told her.

"I couldn't reach my phone and Mr. Brisbane wasn't home, so I couldn't call the school to tell them I wouldn't be in," she explained.

So that's why Principal Morales had been so confused that morning!

"My neighbor finally found me and took me to the hospital. I had to have an operation on my ankle before I could start walking again," she continued. "But of course, it was all *my* fault and not Humphrey's. What did I forget to do, Kelsey?"

"You forgot to pay attention to what you were doing," Kelsey answered.

At least I wasn't *piewhacked* about what had happened anymore! The mystery was solved at last.

I was happy to have our teacher back, but I wished she'd learned to be a ballet dancer instead of breaking her ankle. Ouch!

Mr. E. brought a chair for Mrs. Brisbane, and it was time for Mr. Morales and Mrs. Wright to judge the costumes.

I dove down into my bedding, found my yarn and put on my costume.

Mr. Morales and Mrs. Wright smiled and whispered as they watched my friends parade around the room.

No one was watching me, so to get their attention, I began squeaking loudly.

"SQUEAK-SQUEAK! Look at me!" I repeated over and over.

Finally, Mrs. Brisbane turned to see what was wrong, and she burst out laughing. "What on earth is Humphrey wearing?"

Everyone rushed over to my cage, so I stood up on my rear paws and squeaked some more.

"He's got red yarn on his head," Rosie said.

Thomas leaned in and held up his magnifying glass. "It's red yarn, all right."

Joey leaned in and held up his magnifying glass. "It looks like hair. Red hair."

Kelsey giggled. "He looks like a redhead. From the 'Red-Headed League' story."

I guess it took a redhead to recognize another redhead.

Everyone was laughing and pointing except Mr. Morales and Mrs. Wright. They were whispering and pointing.

"Who gave Humphrey that yarn?" Mrs. Brisbane asked.

No one answered.

"Whoever you are, you're a very clever person," she said.

For once, Mrs. Brisbane was wrong. I am a very clever *hamster*.

Mr. Morales announced that he and Mrs. Wright had made a decision. He reached in his pocket and pulled out a blue ribbon that had Best Costume written on it. "It's a tie between Rosie Rodriguez and . . . Humphrey!"

"BOING-BOING-BOING-BOING!" Og cheered. He knew I'd wanted to win.

Everyone else cheered, too, and Mr. Morales put the ribbon on my cage. He had another Best Costume ribbon, which he gave to Rosie. I was proud to share the honor with her.

"Of course, you're all winners in Room Twenty-six," he said. "Mrs. Brisbane is coming back to teach next week. So I think we should all thank Mr. E. for doing a great job."

He reached in his pocket and pulled out a gold ribbon that had Best Substitute written on it. Mr. E. looked very happy to accept it.

"Now, boys and girls, Mrs. Murch is going on a medical leave next week, so Room Twenty-nine needs a substitute. Do you think I should recommend Mr. E.?"

Everyone cheered wildly—even Mrs. Wright!

Then they passed out treats for everyone—including some sunflower seeds for me.

All I can say is: it was a SUPER-SUPER-SUPER-GREAT-GREAT party!

❧

That night, when Og and I were alone in Room 26, I guess I was the happiest hamster on earth.

I'd made my friends laugh, and I had a shiny blue ribbon on my cage.

My favorite teacher, Mrs. Brisbane, was coming back.

My next-favorite teacher, Ms. Mac, was just down the hall.

My other favorite teacher, Mr. E., would still be at Longfellow School for a while.

And even though I'd just solved a lot of mysteries in Room 26, I knew that as long as I was a hamster living in a classroom full of humans, I'd always have plenty of mysteries to solve . . . just like Sherlock Holmes!

HUMPHREY'S DETECTIONARY: Sometimes even excellent clues can lead you in the wrong direction, but it doesn't really matter if everything ends well and your teacher comes back!

Humphrey's Top 10 Tips
for Beginning Detectives

1. To be a detective, you need to find a mystery to solve. They are everywhere, especially when humans are around. (Humans need a lot of help!)

2. To find the clues you need to solve a mystery, it's important to watch and listen to *everything*. (A cage is a good watching place.)

3. It's also unsqueakably important to write your observations in your notebook. You will also need a pencil or pen. (It's a good idea to hide your notebook behind a mirror or some other secret place.)

4. If you don't understand something—like a mystery word—studying things around it will help you work it out.

5. If you're going to watch and listen, you have to be VERY-VERY-VERY quiet and not make a peep—or a squeak!

6. Some detectives, like Sherlock Holmes, wear funny hats. I'm not sure why. Maybe it makes them think better. But you don't *have* to wear a hat to be a detective.

7. It's important to know when it's safe to go searching for clues, especially when you're going in and out of a cage.

8. One mystery often leads to another. And one solution often leads to another.

9. Never, ever give up! This is a good rule for detectives and everyone else!

10. Read a lot of good mystery stories. They're fun . . . and they make you think!

Humphrey Wants to Meet Everyone's Favorite Pets!

Enter the Humphrey Photo Sweepstakes!

The winner will get a detective kit, a pizza party for friends or classmates, and a collection of Humphrey books! (ARV: $245.00)

See official rules on the next page.

✂ --

Humphrey Photo Sweepstakes Entry Form

Enter for an opportunity to win a detective kit, a pizza party for your friends or classmates, and a collection of Humphrey books!! **Just take a photo of your class pet or personal pet.**

Fill out this entry form (or a photocopy of it) or download and print it from www.penguin.com/humphrey and send it with your photo to:

Penguin Young Readers Group Marketing
Attn: Humphrey National Photo Sweepstakes
345 Hudson Street, 15th Fl.
New York, NY 10014

All entries must be postmarked by 10/24/12 and received by 10/31/12.

Full Name: _____

Age: _____

Mailing Address: _____

_____

Parent or Legal Guardian's Full Name:

_____

Parent or Legal Guardian's Phone Number:

_____

Name of Pet: _____

Official Rules for the
Humphrey National Photo Sweepstakes

NO PURCHASE NECESSARY. A PURCHASE WILL NOT ENHANCE YOUR CHANCES OF WINNING.

Open to residents of the fifty United States and the District of Columbia, ages 7 to 12.

How to Enter:
1. To enter the **Humphrey National Photo Sweepstakes** ("Sweepstakes"), please read these Official Rules and take a photo of a pet you have at home, or your classroom pet. Then fill in the tear-off entry form here or download and print it out from http://www.penguin.com/humphrey. Include your first and last name, the name of your pet, your full mailing address, age, telephone number and the first and last name of your parent or legal guardian. Mail the entry form and photo to: Penguin Young Readers Marketing, 345 Hudson Street, New York, NY 10014, ATTN: **Humphrey National Photo Sweepstakes.** Submissions by fax, email or any other electronic means will not be considered. Limit one entry per person.

2. Sweepstakes begins June 28, 2012. Entries must be postmarked on or before October 24, 2012 and received on or by October 31, 2012. Entries are void if they are in whole or in part illegible, incomplete or damaged. Sponsor assumes no responsibility for late, lost, damaged, incomplete, illegible, postage due or misdirected entries.

3. Penguin Young Readers Group, a division of Penguin Group (USA) Inc. ("Sponsor") and its parent, subsidiary and affiliated companies are not responsible for technical malfunctions of any kind which may limit the ability to play or participate, or by any human error which may occur in the processing of the entries in this Sweepstakes. If for any reason the Sweepstakes is not capable of being conducted as described in these rules, Sponsor shall have the right to cancel, terminate, modify or suspend the Sweepstakes.

Winner:
1. From all eligible entries received, one (1) winner will be chosen in a random drawing held on or about November 15, 2012 by Sponsor, whose decisions concerning all matters related to this Sweepstakes are final and binding.

2. Winner will be notified by telephone. The odds of winning depend on the number of eligible entries received.

Prize:
1. One (1) winner will receive: a set of all the Humphrey books by Betty G. Birney, including *The World According to Humphrey, Friendship According to Humphrey, Trouble According to Humphrey, Surprises According to Humphrey, Adventure According to Humphrey, Summer According to Humphrey, School Days According to Humphrey,* and *Mysteries According to Humphrey* (Approximate Retail Value ("ARV"): $120.00); a detective kit (ARV: $25.00); and a pizza party for his or her friends or classmates (ARV: $100.00). Total ARV of prize: $245.00.

2. In the event that there is an insufficient number of entries Sponsor reserves the right not to award the prize.

Eligibility:
This sweepstakes is open to residents of the fifty United States and the District of Columbia, ages 7-12. Employees of Sponsor, and its parent company, subsidiaries, affiliates, or other parties in any way involved in the development, production or distribution of this Sweepstakes, as well as the immediate family (spouse, parents, siblings, children) and household members of each such employee are not eligible to participate in this Sweepstakes. Void where prohibited by law. All state and local restrictions apply.

General:
1. No substitution, transfers or assignments of prizes allowed. In the event of unavailability, Sponsor may substitute a prize of equal or greater value.

2. All expenses, including taxes (if any), related to receipt and use of prize are the sole responsibility of the winner(s).

3. Winner may be required to execute an Affidavit of Eligibility and Release ("Affidavit") and if so, the Affidavit must be completed and returned within fourteen (14) days of receipt or winner will forfeit the prize and another winner will be selected. If a selected winner is under eighteen (18) years of age, his/her parent or legal guardian will be required to sign the Affidavit. Should the ARV of the prize equal or exceed $600.00, winner shall be required to provide a Social Security Number or a Taxpayer Identification Number to Sponsor for issuance of a 1099 Form.

4. By accepting the prize, winner grants to Sponsor the right to use his/her name, likeness, hometown and biographical information in advertising and promotion materials, including posting on the Sponsor's and author's website, without further compensation or permission, except where prohibited by law.

5. By competing in this Sweepstakes and/or accepting a prize, entrants release Sponsor, its parent, subsidiary or affiliated companies or the advertising agencies of any of them and the authors and/or editors of any books promoted hereby from any and all liability for any loss, harm, injuries, damages, cost or expense arising out of or relating to participation in this Sweepstakes or the acceptance, use or misuse of the prize.

6. Any dispute arising from this Sweepstakes will be determined according to the laws of the State of New York, without reference to its conflict of law principles, and the entrants consent to the personal jurisdiction of the state and federal courts located in New York County and agree that such courts have exclusive jurisdiction over all such disputes.

Winners List:
For a copy of the winners list, send a self-addressed, stamped envelope by March 7, 2013 to: Penguin Young Readers Marketing, 345 Hudson Street, New York, NY 10014, ATTN: **Humphrey National Photo Sweepstakes** Winners List.

Sponsor:
Penguin Young Readers Group
A Division of Penguin Group (USA) Inc.
345 Hudson Street
New York, New York 10014

Photo © Frank Birney

Betty G. Birney has written episodes for numerous children's television shows, including *The New Adventures of Madeline*, *Doug*, and *Bobby's World*, as well as after-school specials and a television movie, *Mary Christmas*. She has won many awards for her television work, including an Emmy, three Humanitas Prizes, and a Writers Guild of America Award.

In addition to the Humphrey books, she is the author of *The Seven Wonders of Sassafras Springs* and *The Princess and the Peabodys*.

A native of St. Louis, Missouri, Betty lives in Los Angeles with her husband, an actor.

Find fun Humphrey activities
and teachers' guides at
www.bettygbirney.com